Movie
Monsters

Edited by

Jonathan W. Thurston

A THURSTON HOWL PUBLICATIONS BOOK

MOVIE MONSTERS

Edited by Thurston Howl
Cover design by Thurston Howl
Cover art by creeps © 2018

First edition, 2019. All rights reserved.

A Thurston Howl Publications Book
Published by Thurston Howl Publications
thurstonhowlpublications.com
Lansing, MI

Movie

Monsters

Contents

Introduction

Welcome to our second volume of the HOWLERS series, *Movie Monsters*. Inspired by all the classics, from Bela Lugosi's *Dracula* and the insect thriller *Them!*, I wanted to see a literary anthology that both celebrated this classic trope as well as transformed it for a 21st century audience that is ever looking to the future. If horror, as numerous scholars have stated, is a reflection of cultural anxieties, what kinds of monsters would stand in for our current problems? For some in this book, it's neo-Nazis. For others, it's dictatorship. For others still, it can often be pure, unadulterated evil. And so, without further ado...

Lights.
Camera.
Action!

Jonathan W. Thurston

B-Train Blues

STEVEN VAN PATTEN

To the handful of people that passed him on the subway platform, Kenneth appeared calm. Unfortunately, he was screaming on the inside. It was a bad mood born from a long day in the office and a recent text message exchange with his girlfriend of six months:

Are you home yet?

No. Been waiting for a train for about 15 min.

It's 10:38. This is the third late night this week. You know what I have been through. If you're seeing other people just be honest with me.

I'm just trying to catch the B train.

I'm sorry to be like this. Get home safe.

Kenneth rolled his eyes. He really wanted things to work with Samantha, but the constant barrage of text messages accusing him of things he had neither the time nor inclination to do was wearing on his patience. In contrast, Samantha's last relationship was with a very charming sex-addict who, to hear her tell it, bedded several 'exotic dancers' in Brooklyn during the run of their relationship. Because of this, the 'working late thing' was putting her on edge.

"And here I thought dating would be easier in my forties," he said under his breath.

As he stood on the platform muddling over the situation, the tracks began to gleam from headlights reflected on the rails as the train he'd been waiting for finally pulled into the Penn Station 34th street station. The breeze brought on by a train as it barreled out of the tunnel was always a welcome sensation.

As the train cars zipped by, it seemed as if everyone else in New York City had the good sense to already be home. Many of the cars contained less than five people. Encouraged by this, he shuffled slightly, scanning the windows with his eyes, hoping to end up in a near empty car like the ones that had already passed. Then, as the train halted, he saw that the second to last car was, in fact, empty.

Jackpot!

At least that's how he saw it. No teenagers dancing and twirling about. No one selling fruit rollups. No musicians. No homeless people. No conmen pretending to be homeless people. Just rows of orange seats and steel poles. He gave a sigh of contentment and sat down.

"This train is making all local stops." Over the train's loudspeaker system, the conductor managed to confirm Kenneth's suspicions regarding how long the trip would take and sound pretty depressed at the same time.

"Might as well get comfortable," Kenneth said to himself as he reached in his blue knapsack for his skinny, white headphones. By the time he untangled them, the train was pulling into the next stop.

If I could just get back all the time in my life I've spent untangling headphones, I'd be a much younger man, he thought as he shook his head in frustration.

At 23rd Street, multiple sets of twin doors opened up, and two much younger men made a mad dash to reach and then hold the doors on the far side of his car as a third member of their party struggled to catch up. Kenneth's teeth grinded as the conductor tried to close the doors to no avail.

"Let go of the car doors in the rear, please." The conductor snapped over the loudspeaker.

"Fuck you!" one of the kids shouted back.

Assholes. Disappointed that three foul-mouthed Abercrombie and Fitch models had invaded his car, he pulled his smartphone out and turned up the volume on his music so he wouldn't have to listen to whatever insipid conversation they were no doubt about to have.

Kenneth glanced over at the three kids and noticed one of them was drinking from a beer can. After a gulp, he passed it around so his two friends could take a swig each. From their body language and their not so alert eyes, Kenneth figured they each had about half a six-pack in them.

Kenneth couldn't help but be irritated. *The cops would have given me and my little dipshit crew an HBO-documentary-inspiring ass-whipping if we were out here with uncovered beer. Assuming these yoyos are headed to Brooklyn, I guess we'll chalk it up to new residents, new rules. What the hell is that kid drinking, anyway? Is that a Foster's. As in 'Foster's... Australian for douchebag.'*

In his ever-growing dismay, he couldn't help but think back to when he was in his early twenties. Back then, his parents would warn about being on the subway at this hour. New York had never been the safest place in the world, but by the time he was old enough to make moves without worrying about a curfew, the five boroughs had become engulfed in a crack epidemic. The subsequent drug war took the lives of many a young black and Latino kid. But that was a long time ago. Now, instead of stepping over crack vials, a kid growing up in Brooklyn stood a better chance of getting artisanal cheese on his shoes.

The fact that they wouldn't sit down while they had their loud conversation gave Kenneth hope that the three screamers might be getting off soon. Five stops later that hope died as not only did the Musketeers not leave, but a woman in a burka boarded the train at the Prince Street Station.

He glanced up quickly, just enough to take notice of her and confirm that she was neither a threat nor someone familiar before going back to facing straight ahead.

The doors closed, and the train rumbled on through the tunnel, making its last stop in Manhattan before plunging into a darkness that led outside and across the Manhattan Bridge. He watched as the skyline whisked by in all of its urban architectural splendor. One of the many magnificent sights available to and therefore taken for granted by Native New Yorkers.

Aggressive music was what usually got him through his subway rides, whether it be old-school rappers like DMX or metal bands like Metallica. In fact, DMX rhythmically pontificating over his rivals being bitch ass niggas that couldn't handle life on the streets or in jail as effectively as he had, was the theme of the song Kenneth had been listening to when the train suddenly halted in the middle of the bridge.

One of the boys said something very loud, prompting Kenneth to turn his head. His lips pressed together in anger as he saw the three idiots were now standing over the woman in the burka. Kenneth had hoped that the drunkards would have kept their shenanigans to themselves and not be the kind of guys who felt empowered to express unwarranted sentiments just because of who might be the current occupant of the White House.

The timing within the music he was listening to became a critical part of the equation, as the DMX song faded and "Nightmare," a well-known track by the band Avenged Sevenfold started with a series of subdued music box chimes before kicking in with heavy metal guitars. The gentle twenty-second intro allowed Kenneth to hear what was being said a few feet away.

"It's sand niggers like you who are ruining our country! Look what happened to my friend!" Douche-Bag said.

"He's kidding, ma'am!" said the one they had held the door for earlier. "I got hurt in a hunting accident. But he does have a point. If your people hate this country so much, that you can't even dress normal while you're here, maybe you shouldn't be here. No offense."

Oh my God, is he trying to be a polite racist?! Kenneth thought as he noticed that the young man was, in fact, wearing a prosthetic arm. Two shiny hooks glistened on the end of the artificial appendage. Kenneth figured he hadn't noticed the prosthetic earlier because he really had been trying to mind his business.

The woman said something, but with the Avenged song kicking in and her face being covered, Kenneth had missed it.

"Folks, we are experiencing a delay. We hope to be moving shortly. We apologize for any inconvenience," the conductor recited in his best 'I want to kill myself' voice.

"Great," Kenneth sighed as he slowly pulled out his ear buds, strapped on his knapsack and stood up. He half-wished he had a weapon instead of a backpack filled with work papers. The boxcutters and nunchakus he used to carry around when he was a teenager would have been great confidence boosters.

"Leave the lady alone!" he said in the most authoritative voice he could muster. It didn't come out as good as he'd hoped. His throat had dried up after two steps forward.

"Mind your business, Denzel!" were the first words Kenneth had heard from the third kid. "You were pretending not to hear us earlier, now all of a sudden you're some fucking hero?"

Oh, so they were talking shit about me? Okay, I got this now.

The woman in the burka turned in his direction, staring at him in what he assumed was gratitude. Even though she was fully covered, Kenneth could see that she was trembling.

"You should probably do as he says, mister," the polite racist suggested. "There are three of us, after all."

"I count two and three-quarters," Kenneth retorted as he pointed toward the plastic appendage. "What happened? You lose your arm prepping for the weekly cross burning?"

"I'll have him tear your fucking throat out, you nosy, uppity black piece of shit," Douche Bag shouted as he pointed at his friend's hooks.

As the boys stepped forward, various scenarios flashed in Kenneth's mind. One where the train pulls into Brooklyn just in time for new passengers to find his lifeless body lying next to the Muslim lady's. Another where a cop is delivering the bad news to friends or family. Still a third vision had him surviving the fight only to end up being blamed for the whole thing and arrested. Yet and still, he couldn't have sat there in good conscience and just let these dumb boys rail on a defenseless woman. He hadn't been raised like that.

Kenneth half-expected Douche Bag to throw the beer can, so when it came hurtling at his head, Kenneth was able to dodge it with a quick jerk to the left. Droplets of beer splattered across the left side of his jacket as the Third Guy made his way over and swung at him. A grazing blow across Kenneth's chin. It had been forever since anyone had dared to attempt to punch him in the face and for a brief moment, the world seemed to slow down. With all the strength he could muster, he shoved Third Guy hard into Douche Bag, sending them both tumbling to the train car floor. By the time he turned to Polite Racist it was too late. Hardened plastic struck Kenneth on the side of his face, cutting in a scar and a creating a bruise across his cheek as he was knocked backward.

Kenneth fought to stay conscious and get back to his feet.

As he reeled, he noticed the woman's shuddering had turned to full-on convulsions. There was another noise, as if the burka were ripping.

Ah, don't tell me these racist assholes are right, and this woman is about to blow us up!

Polite Racist stood over Kenneth, seemingly to deliver another blow to his head, when the woman screamed loud enough for his eardrums to vibrate. As the scream continued, it morphed into a roar. Animalistic. Guttural. Primal. The entire train car shook. Polite Racist turned towards the sound, which gave Kenneth the chance to kick the boy in the groin, sending him falling back towards his friends.

The center of the burka ripped open. Naked breasts all but shriveled as they turned from brown and supple to furry and grey. As the rest of the outfit fell away, a fang-filled snout pushed out from the lady's face. Her now exposed arms went through the same change the chest had, as maple syrup colored human skin gave way to more icy grey fur and lupine features.

As the transformation continued, the three young men who once considered themselves to have the advantage, were now in full retreat. Terrified and tripping over each other like a bad vaudeville act, they made it to the opposite side of the train car, only to find the door locked. Trapped, they banged on the glass and metal door, screaming for help as they tried to get the attention of the people in the next car.

Kenneth couldn't tell if their efforts were working or not. Along with his view being obstructed by the boys themselves, he found himself distracted by the she-wolf, whose legs and torso he watched expand until she stood at nearly six-foot-two.

At this point, Kenneth was actually closest to the creature and could only pray she'd turn her attention to the boys first. He was hit by an odd sense of hope as the werewolf snarled at him, then whipped her head back towards the twenty-somethings and roared.

As she took two steps toward them, Kenneth slowly picked himself up that and ran to the door on his side, despite the red, black and white 'No Exit' sign.

Kenneth tried his door to no avail, but only stopped pulling when the screaming began anew. He turned to see the she-wolf smack Third Guy and Polite Racist out of her way and bear down on Douche Bag. As his two friends tried to recover from her assault, she pushed the young beer connoisseur down to the floor and squatted down over him. A clawed hand braced itself against the young man's chest and squeezed and pulled until blood began to seep through his white t-shirt.

They all heard a sort of squelch that normally accompanies the fleshy part of a left pectoral muscle being torn from someone's body. Douche Bag cried out like a man on fire, but not for long. In a fashion similar to a lion on the Serengeti, she leaned in with her gruesome mouth and bit down hard enough to snap the boy's neck. A few more biting motions, and the boy's head was dislodged. Blood flowed in gushes, creating a pool under the lifeless body and staining the beast's grey fur.

Kenneth continued his futile pulling and banging. Every last person in the next car had their heads down and their earbuds inserted. Two of them were fast asleep. There'd be no help coming from that direction.

More screams from behind him. Kenneth looked over his shoulder again, just in time to see the monster raise her arm and slap Third Guy hard enough to spin his head 180 degrees. The boy was dead before he hit the floor with five deep gashes running diagonally across his face.

The werewolf turned just as Polite Racist found his feet. For some reason that's probably tied to how the bigoted man-child lost his arm, he was still as calm as when he had been berating the wolf's human form with Federalist logic.

A whirring sound filled the train car as the snarling werewolf stepped forward. Across the way, Kenneth marveled as the two hooks on the end of the prosthetic arm straightened then bent outwards and began spinning like blades in a food processor.

Kenneth's eyes widened with disbelief as Polite Racist stepped in front of the werewolf, brandishing the prosthetic and it's spinning blades as if he were Zorro about to duel the evil Alcalde.

Fuck this. I've gotta be dreaming. Or high. Did someone give me 'shrooms' while I was at work?

Kenneth continued to watch as the werewolf lunged, giving Polite Racist a clear shot at her face. Quick reflexes seemed to be the only thing that stopped the beast from getting half of her snout ripped off. She howled in pain and retreated as droplets of blood fell from her jaw to the already crimson-stained floor.

Polite Racist took a step forward. The wolf backed up. Kenneth's eyes widened as the bizarre dance continued for another three steps, slowly bringing the fight closer to him. The wolf growled, while the other combatant managed to find his voice and finally betray his emotions.

"You killed my friends, you fucking Muslim bitch!" he said as he swung his mechanized weapon at her again, only to miss as she bounced just out of the way. "Everything Fox says about you people is true! You're all a bunch of perverse fucking demons! I can't wait to tell the world about you so we can send our troops in and annihilate whatever fucking country you're from!"

The kid sprung forward and took a swing that was wider and far less cautious than any of his previous attempts, forcing the werewolf to duck. Seeing her almost on the floor made him think he had her. He raised the propeller end of his prosthetic high over his head, clearly believing this was the moment for a death blow. It would have been a terrible head wound for the werewolf had he not misjudged the angle. In the end, the blow got caught in one of the train car poles.

The werewolf sprang up quickly from her crouched position and jabbed a clawed hand deep into boy's abdomen. Then, the second blood-stained claw hand dug in and kept digging. She pulled out the boy's innards, splashing blood all over the floor and any orange and yellow seats close by.

On the other side of the car, Kenneth clasped a hand over his mouth. He was repressing a scream and vomit. But an odd noise did escape his throat as the most disgusting thing he'd ever seen played out a few feet away.

Polite Racist finally crumbled to the floor and lay in a pool of slimy red things that used to be inside of him. As a finisher, the werewolf raised an angled leg and stomped on the prosthetic arm twice, silencing it as effectively as she had the owner.

The train still hadn't moved and for at least a minute, neither did the werewolf. Was she resting? Figuring out her next move? It was hard to tell. Meanwhile, Kenneth had not moved and was barely breathing.

Maybe now that she's killed these guys, she'll calm down and change back. You know, like the Hulk. I just have to wait for her to get to her quiet place.

That's when his cellphone dinged with a text message alert. Probably Samantha making sure he hadn't detoured into a bar or an ex-girlfriend's place before going home. Instinctively, his hand dove into his pocket to silence the phone, but it was too late. If the werewolf had forgotten about Kenneth, that ping noise had served as the reminder.

She turned around slowly, baring her blood-stained fangs.

"Ah, fuck," he said under his breath as the growling started again. Despite his heart beating hard in his chest, he found his authoritative voice for the second time since he'd gotten on this cursed train. "Hey look! I was trying to help you!"

The werewolf took her first step towards him.

"Wait! Come on! Not only should you let me go, you should..."

The creature roared at him as it shortened the distance between them with two long strides.

"Yo! Seriously, I do not deserve this! What're you fittin' to do, anyway? Eat me? I'm not Halal! You know? This is so fucked up!"

Despite his protests, she continued stepping forward, leaving bloody paw-foot prints in her wake.

"This is not right!" Kenneth shouted, his voice cracking under the weight of the fear rising in him. All the declaration did was prompt another roar. She was right on him now, towering over him as he began to cower. He let out a final scream as a bloody paw-hand raised up to the train car roof. There would be no pole to obstruct this blow as it came crashing down.

Kenneth gasped as he came to. His mind and body were reacting to the last moments he remembered; the drunk Nazi Youth group getting murdered and his nearly being killed by something he didn't' even believe in. His heart was racing and didn't slow down until he realized that he was home. And not just home, but lying on his back in his bed, still in his clothes, with his backpack next to him.

A nightmare? That was a nightmare? But no, it felt too fucking real. Plus, my entire head hurts. And why are my clothes wet?

He sat up and looked around his modest one-bedroom apartment. Even with the lamps off he could see that nothing was damaged or out of place. Seconds later, it dawned on him that if the digital clock on his nightstand was correct, he stood incapable of accounting for roughly two hours.

One thirty-six AM! What the fuck?

He reached for the lamp next to the digital clock, which

clicked on and sent hot yellow light across the bedroom and to a lesser degree, through the bedroom door and into his living room and connected kitchen area.

Anxiety filled his belly as the sound of the front door locks tumbling open filled his ears. It could only be one person. Samantha had insisted they trade apartment keys a month ago, with the understanding that the keys would only be used in emergencies. Her presence meant that two hours of unanswered phone calls constituted an emergency. He swung his legs off the side of the bed and braced himself for the verbal bitch-slapping he was about to receive.

Samantha was dressed in an expensive-looking sweat suit and NIKE sneakers. Still pretty as ever. With her hair in a ponytail, she looked almost as good as she did angry.

"So you're not dead? Just an inconsiderate bastard! You— you do know that, right?" Samantha slammed the door behind her and stormed across the apartment into the bedroom as he rose to his feet. "I've been calling and texting you for hours! Do you have any idea how worried I was about you? Why are you still dressed? Did you just get here after you told me you were going home hours ago? Did you not hear about the white boys that got killed on the subway this evening? Around the same damn time I thought you were on the train and on the same damn train line you usually take!"

"Honey, I'm sorry," Kenneth held his hands up in surrender. "I got here, and I guess I must have passed out."

"Bullshit! And why are your clothes wet? Are you on drugs?"

He considered telling her the truth, but if she found 'I got home and fell asleep' to be disingenuous, there was no telling how she would take 'I got caught in the middle of a werewolf attack and really don't remember how I got home'.

"Samantha! Baby! I didn't mean to worry you. I swear, I just..."

"And what happened to your face?"

"I must have fallen." He mentally patted himself on the back for the quick lie.

"If you fell, why aren't you in a gutter somewhere? See! Drugs! Or someone hit you because you were doing something you had no business doing. Don't remember how you got home, my ass!"

"Look, Samantha—"

"And see! This is the other thing. How am I supposed to believe you take this relationship seriously when you don't include me in your big decisions?"

"Big decisions? What are you talking about? What big decision?"

"When were you going to tell me you got a fucking dog?"

"A what?" He realized that she was angrily glaring at something behind him and turned around slowly. Crouched down low next to the foot of his bed was the werewolf. A king-sized quilt that had been on the bed before he'd left for work was partially covering her. The beast's more humanoid features were hidden, but it was easy to see that she was still quite large. The creature's eyes darted back and forth between the two, but she made no hostile moves.

"Look at the size of this thing! First of all, I don't even like dogs! And I really don't like ones big enough to kill you in your sleep."

Shit, if she only knew!

Samantha suddenly shook her head so violently that for a moment, Kenneth thought she was transforming. "That's it! I can't take it anymore. You don't respect me, and you don't care about me, or this relationship. This is over!"

"Samantha, that's simply not true!" was all he could muster.

"Whatever!"

A feeling of helplessness washed over him. Any thoughts he had on saving the troubled romance all but died at that moment. The way he saw it, he could walk over to the foot of the bed and pull the blanket off the beast and blow Samantha's mind, but there is no telling how she'd react or what she would want to do. Plus, did the werewolf want Samantha to know she wasn't a large Siberian Husky? Would the reaction to full disclosure be to murder him and Samantha? There was no way to answer these questions, so he watched quietly as Samantha grabbed her things from various closets and dresser drawers and shoved them into a Duane Reade shopping bag. Then she threw his keys on the kitchen table.

"Give me my keys!" she shouted at him. He quickly fished into his pocket and produced them. She walked over and snatched the keys out of his hand. Then, she gave him one last forlorn look before she marched across and out of the apartment with the same vigor and pace with which she had burst in.

As the door slammed shut, Kenneth sat back down on the bed. After a moment, the werewolf pushed off the quilt, stood up from where she'd been curled up on the floor and sat down next to him.

"Thanks for bringing me home," he said. He was still unnerved by all this, but clearly an understanding had been reached.

The werewolf nodded, then barked and whined as her snout turned in his direction.

He could only assume she was trying to say something. "What?" he finally asked.

The werewolf pointed at the front door.

"Oh. Samantha? Don't worry about that. Now that I'm thinking on it, we were doomed. It's okay."

The werewolf gave one final whimper, then fell silent.

"You thirsty?" he asked after a minute.

The werewolf nodded again and seconds later, they were in his kitchen standing on either side of the same table where

Samantha had just left his spare keys. He drank from a coffee mug and had provided his guest with a Teenaged Mutant Ninja Turtle cereal bowl. Ironically, Samantha hated that bowl.

"Let's see if I understand this. You were never going to kill me. You just needed me to shut up."

The werewolf stopped lapping and splashing water just long enough to nod.

"And you didn't leave me on the train because you knew I'd probably get blamed for the murders."

A nod and a shrug followed. Kenneth almost laughed.

"And one would worry about bloody werewolf prints leading the cops to this apartment, except you're clean and my clothes are wet. Safe to assume that after you got us off the train, you found water somewhere and cleaned us up?"

A very enthusiastic nod.

"But how did you know where my place is?"

The werewolf turned and walked back to the bedroom. When she came out she was holding his wallet. She put it on the table and went back to the water.

Kenneth put down the cup and picked up the wallet. After a quick rifling he found his driver's license with a single bloodstain smeared across it.

Kenneth turned to the kitchen sink and started cleaning the license with dish soap and a rag.

"You are going to change back at some point, yes?" he asked over his shoulder.

The werewolf yipped. Somehow, it came across as a 'yes'.

"Great," he sighed. "I'll go find you a new burka in the morning."

As he glanced back at her again, the she-wolf looked as if she were trying to smile at him, as a way of saying, 'thank you' for his thoughtfulness. "Well, at least I made one woman happy tonight," he said under his breath as he finished wiping the blood off of the license.

Encounter with the River God

CLINT COLLINS

Julie Reed lay on the sundeck of the seventy-five foot luxury sport yacht as it headed upriver, stretching out long legs and reading the latest research on climate change and its effect on fish populations in the Amazon.

"More water, Señorita Reed?" A smiling crewman held a large glass pitcher in which slices of lemons floated like yellow lilies.

"*Por favor*," said Julie, holding out her glass. Enrique tried extra hard to make sure he didn't spill a single drop, even though it was exceedingly difficult not to stare at the full breasts just barely contained by the skimpy bikini top.

"*Obrigada*," said Julie, thanking him as he topped off her glass. Enrique allowed himself a quick glance into her cleavage where little drops of sweat glistened. He was sure they tasted like nectar.

A minute later up the stairs came her Indian guide and interpreter. The same age as Julie, she also wore a bikini, bought at the same store in Manaus before they got on the boat.

"Any river pirates today, Maira?" Julie spoke to her in Portuguese, a language she had studied since her first year in college.

The woman, whose long dark hair fell to her waist, shook her head. "No, we've passed that dangerous section of the river between Coari and Codajás, but it gets worse each year."

Maira took a sip of her Bohemia beer and scanned the river ahead of them before taking a seat on one of the couches. Pirates on speedboats would love to come after this nice yacht, take it over, and kill everyone on board. She had heard they cut the intestines out of the bodies so they wouldn't float, then pitched the dead and their guts into the river. Of course, they would certainly take their time raping her and Julie before taking the machete to them.

"How far are we from the village?" Julie sat up and applied more suntan oil to her legs and arms. Working on her doctorate in ichthyology often meant long days in the library or lab, so it was good to finally get some sunshine on her pale body.

Maira looked at the dense jungle on both sides of the river. It all seemed the same to Julie, so she had to smile when Maira folded heavily tattooed arms and closed her eyes for a moment.

When she opened them, she said, "Just before sunset we will be at *Lagoa Negra.*"

The Black Lagoon.

Julie stood and let the wind fly in her dark hair, wondering if her grandmother had seen the same bamboo groves along the banks on her trip up the Amazon sixty-five years ago.

Now it was her turn.

Julie reached for her water. Could she really help the secluded Indian village like her grandmother did? Would she have the same strength Kay Lawrence had at her age so long ago?

She took a deep breath and felt Maira's hand on her arm.

"You will be doing a good thing, my sister. Do not worry. The village will be so happy to see you."

Julie squeezed Maira's hand, writhing with esoteric art, and sat back down. The intricate tattoos all along the woman's body meant she was the village shaman. Had been since she was five years old and waded into the lagoon and sang, without ever knowing the words, the summoning song for their river god.

There was definitely magic working in Maira, Julie had to admit, as the Indian knew her moods even before she did.

Maira turned to see the boat's captain coming up the stairs, her face impassive.

"Señoritas," said Luiz, the skipper and owner of the *Rita,* "how are you this afternoon?"

Maira turned to look at the river.

"*Ola,* Luiz." Julie put out her hand, and the captain shook it with both of his and took a seat across from her, giving him a good view of the bosom Julie always felt was a little too generous.

"Looking forward to seeing the lagoon? I've never been myself, but both my grandfather and father have said it is beautiful." Luiz gave her his most charming smile and relaxed against the couch.

On many of his cruises for rich tourists he could usually count on a bored wife or girlfriend willing to have at least one—more than one if he was lucky—passionate rendezvous with him, very often right here on the sundeck late at night under a world of stars.

But he knew there was no way he would get between the pretty American's thighs with the Indian woman around. She stayed shadow-close, and they often had meals together in their cabin. Maira did all the cooking and used only the food they brought when they came on board.

Julie followed his gaze as the boat approached a bend. "Yes, I can't wait to see it. My grandmother often talked about it, telling me these wonderful stories about the village there. Coming back here, I'm fulfilling one of her last wishes."

"Last wishes? Did Señora Reed pass away?"

Julie nodded. "Yes, last year, in February. She wanted some of her ashes spread in the lagoon."

Luiz swallowed. "I never met my grandfather: he died before I was born, but my father said he often spoke of your grandmother, how beautiful and fearless she was."

"*Obrigada*, Luiz. Kay told me so much about Lucas, too, how he loved the river." Julie touched his arm. "And I like how you kept the name *Rita* for your boat. Very nice."

The mention of his grandmother's name made him smile. "Yes, it's a family tradition now. My father named his charter fishing boat *Rita*."

Maira suddenly stood, walked to the front of the sundeck, and looked upriver. Closing her eyes, she raised a hand to feel the breeze.

Luiz stared at the intricate tattoos swirling on the Indian's legs and arms. Her long hair hid most of the illustrations on her back, but even across her belly swam odd creatures and twisted symbols, Luiz couldn't contain a smile. She wasn't bad to look at, but he couldn't imagine her naked in his bed.

"Something's ahead," Maira said, turning to face them. "But they don't want you...or the boat. No need to get your guns."

Luiz nodded. He had no doubt the Indian woman was right. She had correctly predicted the weather since they left Manaus and told them where to find the mislaid room keys. Crazy tattoos or not, when she spoke he listened.

Julie got to her feet, shaded her eyes, and squinted against the bright sun as she tried to see what was around the turn in the river. "If they don't want us or the boat, what do they want?"

"The River God." Maira sat down but kept her eyes straight ahead.

"You mean the Gill-man?" Luiz looked over the side of the boat just in case the amphibious humanoid some also called "the Creature" was swimming alongside his yacht. Lucas told stories about the monster many years ago to his family, but Luiz never really thought he'd ever see it.

"My tribe doesn't call him that," said Maira, "but I believe that's what they're hoping to find."

"But why are they looking for him out here and not in the lagoons?" asked Julie, scanning the riverbank for any sign of the reclusive "fish-man."

After taking a long pull at her beer, Maira said, "There are people from my village with them. They know I can call the River God to me."

Luiz shook his head. "I better get downstairs and arm the crew. You two ought to go to your cabin. This could get ugly."

As he turned to go down the stairs, Maira caught his wrist. "It will be fine, Luiz. They have no idea what to expect. Just tell your crew not to be alarmed. Let me handle this."

Luiz nodded and went down the stairs toward the *Rita's* bridge where he kept the automatic weapons. He'd long ago gotten the required permits for the guns as river pirates were getting more violent, armed now with AR-15 assault rifles and machineguns. Cruises were getting canceled, hurting villages along the river dependent on the tourist trade. The economic pressure was even forcing some villagers to join the pirates.

Taking the wheel in the cockpit, Luiz could see the large fishing boat anchored in their way as they came around the bend, men on the bow bristling with rifles. He could make a run for it, but they would surely open fire.

The pirates gave a few warning shots in the air, and Luiz slowed the *Rita*, coming alongside the vessel looking a lot like the charter boat stolen last month from a marina at Itacoatiara east of Manaus.

Luiz picked up the megaphone he used to hail passing watercraft. "What can I help you with?"

A young man wearing a necklace of small monkey skulls stepped to the side of his boat. "Let me talk to Maira. We don't want to hurt anyone, unless we have to, but we must talk to her."

Maira stood up from the sundeck and spoke to the man in their tribal language. "Do you really want me to call the River God to you, Davi? Do you not fear his wrath?"

Davi laughed and held up his Beretta M12 submachine gun taken from a Brazilian Army squad that ventured too far into the jungle one day in search of pirates. "I think your river god should fear my bullets." The Indian fired a burst into the water. "Your god is just a big fish, and you have cursed our village with your superstitions."

Davi gestured to the back of the boat. "I want to see if your god is stronger than our nets."

"You are making a mistake, Davi. Turn away now, or I cannot be responsible for what happens to you and your crew. The piranhas will feast on what remains of them."

Julie stirred on the floor of the sundeck behind Maira, and the shaman motioned with her hand below the railing for her to stay low. If the pirates got a look at the beautiful American they might forget all about pursuing their water monster.

"Maira, listen to me." Davi put down his gun and raised his hands to her. "You can make us all very rich and help our village. The old ways are gone. We live in a new time now and there are people who will pay us more money than you can imagine if we catch your creature."

Maira shook her head. "Do not make me do this. If you really want to die here, I will ask you not be mutilated so your mother can see your body."

Davi grabbed his submachine gun and pointed it directly at her. "Summon your fish-man, witch!"

Maira bowed her head, took a deep breath, then looked up to the blue sky above her, raising her arms, and began to sing.

It was a much longer song than Maira usually sang for the Summoning, as she had so much to say. Only the shaman could sense the swirling beneath the boat when she stopped singing.

"I can still stop this, Davi, but you must tell me quickly." Maira looked down into the river. "You don't have much time."

Davi laughed, waved at the village shaman dismissively, and shouted to his men to get the nets ready. "We have the biggest fish in the Amazon to catch today! *Obrigado*, Maira!"

Maira felt the change in the current. "I am sorry, Davi. They are angry now, and I cannot stop them."

"Them?" Davi grinned. "This is a good day indeed!"

A crewman shouted as a black head surfaced, webbed claws rising out of the water. "There! Cast the net there!"

The creature disappeared into the murky water while near the bow of the boat another monster broke the water, head and arms blood-red. Next to it rose one the color of the sky, then both sank and reappeared by the stern. Crewmen rushed from one side of the boat to the other as different Gill-men, each having their own distinctive coloring and markings, bobbed and swam around the fishing boat.

When a golden-scaled water creature appeared by the side of the boat, Davi saw his chance.

"Throw the net! I want that one! The gold one!"

The crewmen pitched the heavy weighted net overboard, but soon realized their mistake. Other creatures swimming nearby leapt upon the net and used it to quickly scramble on board.

The creatures, each about six and a half feet tall, wasted no time once on the boat. The large clawed hands swiped fast and hard across faces, necks, and bellies, and soon the deck was slippery with blood and severed entrails.

So many creatures were now on board no pirate had time to fire his gun, quickly finding a fish-man looming over him, cheek-gills pulsing, black eyes unblinking and merciless, and serrated teeth showing as the thick lips parted.

Once the pirates were shredded to nothing more than

bleeding bags of bones, the creatures lifted their victims over their heads and threw them into the river, where they disappeared into a boiling frenzy of piranha.

Davi was saved for last, trapped on the bow of the boat. Turning to plead to Maira, he saw she was no longer on the sundeck. One creature, jungle-green with yellow slashes on his sides, wrapped strong arms around the villager and jumped into the water.

A day later his drowned but unblemished body washed upon the banks of the Black Lagoon.

One by one the creatures dove off the bloodstained boat, leaving it to drift with the current like some boat that had just arrived from Hell.

Down in their cabin, Julie watched the last of the Gill-men dive into the river. "Where did they all come from, Maira?"

"Some villages still have their own River God, like mine. Others lost theirs when they changed and took up modern ways, and their gods had to swim away and find their brothers."

"They all seemed to get here pretty quickly, lucky for us."

Maira smiled. "One by one they've been with us since we left Manaus, just to protect you."

When the *Rita* sailed into the dark waters of the Black Lagoon an hour later, Julie gave Luiz a hug. "Come back for me in eleven months. No sooner, okay?"

Luiz kissed her on the cheek. "Be careful, señorita. You saw what those man-fish can do."

Julie squeezed his arm. "Don't worry, *meu amigo*. I have no plans to do anything to make them mad, just do my research, and Maira will be with me all the time."

A final hug and she went down the ladder into the canoe the villagers sent for her and their shaman. Luiz waved, backing the boat out of the lagoon, wondering if he would ever see the lovely American again.

The villagers were already dancing when Julie and Maira

stepped out of the canoe. It was sunset, and ceremonial fires had been lit.

"These are your private quarters," said Maira, leading Julie to a thatched hut separate from the village and close to the lagoon. "Get undressed, and I will be right back."

Julie nodded and put her two bags on the dirt floor. There were a couple torches for light and a collection of animal skins on the ground that passed for a bed. Other than a few wooden benches there was nothing in the hut.

Sitting under one of the torches for light, Julie searched in a bag and pulled out the letter her grandmother wrote her not long before her death. She had read it over and over on the boat, smiling at the words of love and encouragement. It felt good to hold those words in her hands now she was in the village at long last.

After reading it three times, Julie tucked it in her bag and began unbuttoning her blouse. She unhooked her bra, and her nipples hardened as much from excitement as from exposure to the evening air. She stood and slid off her shorts and panties and carefully folded everything before putting it all in her suitcase.

Sitting naked on the bench, Julie ran her hands down her belly and along her thighs. She had been preparing for this night since her eighteenth birthday when her grandmother told her everything about her adventure with the Gill-man.

She heard what really happened, not the "official" story that her grandmother was abducted. Kay had been swimming in the Black Lagoon when a school of red-bellied piranha attacked her. Bitten all over her body and in danger of dying, as she was too far from the boat for anyone to hear her screams, Kay was rescued when a man-fish appeared and drove the piranha away.

The Amazon water-creature carried the bleeding Kay to the Indian village where they treated her multiple wounds. An Indian later rowed out to the *Rita*, a tramp steamer captained by Luiz's grandfather, and told Kay's colleague and boyfriend, Dr. David Reed, where she could be found.

Kay decided to recover at the Indian village, and Dr. Reed continued to do his research on fish in the Amazon. As the village women tended to Kay's wounds one day, she learned from them how their river god, the creature that had saved her, was always a dying breed as only males were born.

"How do they reproduce?" Kay had asked.

"We wait for a chosen one to come," said one of the older women brewing for Kay a medicinal tea made from plants in the rainforest. "It is forbidden for women from our tribe to join with our god. We—and he—must wait until his mate arrives."

"For as long as the tribe has lived by the lagoon, since the beginning of the river," said another, putting an ointment on Kay's bites, "we have been protected by our River God, but our women could give him no children. Those that tried died."

"So the tribe prayed to all our gods, and waited," said the priestess combing Kay's dark hair. "And one day a woman did appear, and every generation when it is time for the new River God to mate, a beautiful woman will come to us, like a flower, like rain, and save our tribe and our god."

Kay looked at the priestess and smiled. "I am the one this time, aren't I?"

The three women stayed silent until one of them said, "Only you can decide that. You must choose it, want it."

Kay gestured to her healing wounds. "He saved my life. When you say I'm ready, let me help you—and him."

And on her eighteenth birthday, Julie listened as her grandmother told the tale of the Gill-man, then took her hands and said, "Your grandfather understood what I was doing, and agreed. In ten years, when you're the age I was in the Amazon, you too, if you wish, can go to the Black Lagoon."

There was a knock at the hut's door made of river reeds, and Julie opened it to see Maira holding an ornate tray made of fishbones. On it were three bowls of sacred paint. Behind the shaman Julie could see villagers dancing around three ceremonial bonfires.

Maira stepped inside, and as Julie closed the door she could hear chanting and drumming begin.

"I was told these were the same bowls used when your grandmother was here." Maira motioned for Julie to sit on the bed of animal skins and laid the tray next to them.

The shaman dipped a brush into the first bowl and began painting symbols on Julie's cheeks and forehead. "Blue is for the sky and your beauty which is a gift to us from the gods."

She used another brush for a different bowl. "Red is the fire of passion." Julie looked down as Maira drew crimson designs on her breasts, belly, and thighs.

"Green is for the river and the god it brought us." Julie held out her arms as Maira painted spiraling tribal markings from her wrists to her shoulders. "Could you stand for me?"

Julie stood, and the young shaman painted more sacred symbols up and down the woman's long legs. "I'll do your back now." Julie felt cool brushstrokes on her skin as Maira painted the intricate characters signifying she was the chosen of the River God.

The door opened, and three priestesses of the River God came in, one with the hide of a black jaguar, one with a basket of red orchid petals, and one with a large wooden bowl of water. They spread out the jaguar hide in the center of the hut, then sprinkled red petals over it and in a circle around it. The bowl was set not far from the hide. They bowed wordlessly to the pretty American and left as quietly as they came.

"You are giving us a great gift," said Maira as she stood by the door with her tray and bowls.

"I know I would not be here if the River God had not saved Kay. It is my honor to give myself, to do what I can for you and your tribe." Julie took a deep breath. "I'm ready."

"Food and more water will be brought to you for the next three days, of course. I will sing to summon the River God, and when you hear the chanting stop it means he is here." Maira touched her friend's brightly painted arm. "Thank you, my sister," she said, and closed the door behind her, now decorated with red orchids.

Julie knelt on the black jaguar skin and shivered from both nervousness and excitement. On the boat Maira told her what to expect. The River God would come to her for three nights, leaving just before sunrise each day.

Of course, her grandmother told her the important details. The sex, she had said, would be like nothing else she would ever experience. The claws on the webbed hands would retract and the Gill-man's touch would be smooth and gentle. The Creature's full lips would kiss and taste every inch of her, and the elaborate and tender ritual of lovemaking would last for hours. Kay told her she would come to accept no human man would ever be able to satisfy her like the River God.

Nights with the worshiped man-fish would leave her blissfully exhausted, and the River God's seed would bring strange dreams and hallucinations. Maira told her it was not uncommon to be visited by the spirits of women who laid with a River God, so it was quite possible her grandmother could appear to her. It was all part of welcoming her to a very exclusive sisterhood.

Julie could hear Maira singing in her high lovely voice, the chanting growing louder. The villagers formed a circle around a naked woman, painted like Julie but without certain symbols, and a man painted green. They danced closely, but not yet allowed to touch.

When the chanting stopped, Julie lay back on black fur and red flowers, heart pounding. The hut door soon opened and closed, and a Gill-man, taller than she expected and blackish-green like the depths of the lagoon, walked slowly toward her, erection clearly visible in the torchlight.

Julie opened her arms and spoke the words of welcome Maira taught her in the ancient tribal language.

"Come to me, son of the river. Take what is yours."

Singing a different song, Maira walked out into the waters of the lagoon, holding a small urn. She kept singing, standing in water up to her hips, until another man-fish surfaced. This one was greenish-gray and moved with some effort as he came toward her.

Claws trembling, the aged Gill-man took the urn from Maira and walked slowly away until he disappeared beneath the dark water. Once down near the bottom of the lagoon, the Gill-man opened the urn and freed the white ashes.

As they swirled around him, the old man-fish remembered how he and Kay swam together in a sun-dappled lagoon as her belly grew.

She had been his only love, lost for all these years.

Now she was home again.

In memory of Julie Adams, who portrayed Kay Lawrence in "The Creature From the Black Lagoon."

The Thing that Goes Bump in the Night

REBECCA ROWLAND

Penny surreptitiously glanced at her watch: it was only six o'clock. It was late winter, and the dying sunlight drizzled languidly through the window. A half-naked maple tree danced drunkenly on the lawn outside. Penny could hear the shrieks of children playing somewhere nearby; these were children from the neighboring homes that stayed warm and toasty from October through April and bundled themselves in blankets of fresh, green lawns from May through September.

She herself lived in a poor but eerily quiet district of the city. The nearest house was a good ten-minute walk down the road; she never thought to draw her curtains at night, although the draftiness forced her to cover her windows with plastic sheeting each year, making her feel like a strange bug being slowly cocooned. Once upon a time, Penny had ambitions of wealth, but those were soon dashed, and it was just as well.

It wasn't that Brian Shea was a difficult patient. He was generally agreeable, fought her only on the rare occasion that he was under the weather or cranky, and most nights, he was perfectly content to lie in bed, staring blankly at the television on his bureau, binge-watching a comedy series or police procedural without any conversation. That was the hardest part of her job, as far as Penny was concerned: keeping the mindless chatter going day after day. But Brian kept to himself more often than not, and she had grown relatively comfortable to the silence that grew between them each evening as the sun set.

As a licensed nurse, Penny would have gleaned a more lucrative salary had she selected a position in a hospital or physician's practice, but working as a caretaker provided her with a more tranquil schedule and much less paperwork. Her last client had been a woman in her eighties named Stella Lewandowski. Stella had a mild case of dementia, and Penny had worked the day shift then, eight in the morning until five at night, escaping the worst of her client's confusion just as the sun began to disappear and her relief arrived to take over. Penny had her own demons at home, and an overnight run seemed like a good opportunity to refocus them, so when Stella finally passed—her frail, powdery body discovered in an awkward clump on the floor next to the bed one stormy afternoon—Penny specifically requested an evening shift for her next placement, and her tour with Brian began.

Brian Shea was atypical of her standard clientele. A robust man in his early forties, he was broad-shouldered and athletic with a handsome, square jaw, and he worked as a systems analyst for a financial planning agency in the city. After a bizarre snowboarding accident while on holiday in Glen Shee a month ago, Brian had been frustrated to learn he'd be bed-ridden at home for at least ten weeks with two broken legs and a fractured wrist. He was a life-long bachelor, and with no family to care for him full-time, he'd hired a nurse to tend to him during the days while he telecommuted to work, often wearing a custom-tailored dress shirt and tie over a pair of boxer shorts to engage in corporate Skype meetings in front of his laptop's webcam. It wasn't until the night terrors began that Brian decided to hire an overnight nurse to stay with him.

The first one had happened out of the blue. He awoke disorientated, gasping for breath as he stared at the blue digital numbers on his alarm clock. Two o'clock. His sheets were soaked with sweat, and the skin on his back felt chafed and tender from lying in the quickly cooling wetness. There was a loud pounding on the door in the kitchen as Brian blinked furiously, trying to recall where he was and what had happened. The room was dark, darker than he could ever remember it being. It was only when he tried to climb out of bed that he remembered the two casts weighing down the lower half of his body.

"Fuck!" he cried out in frustration. The knocking stopped. A moment later, Brian's cell phone rang, the illuminated screen casting an alien glow over his nightstand. He grabbed the phone and tapped the green ANSWER icon. "Hello?"

"Mr. Shea? Brian? It's Jade from next door," said a small voice. "I...we heard you screaming and...and I just wanted to check that you were alright," she explained. "I'm sorry if I startled you. I know it's very late."

Screaming? He hadn't remembered screaming, but now that he was speaking out loud, his throat felt raw. "Yes," he began, "yes, Jade, I'm fine. Just a nightmare, I suppose."

Jade was quiet, and for a moment, Brian wondered if she'd hung up. Then she said, "Oh, alright...I was just concerned because...well, with three broken bones, you can never be too careful, you know, about the possibility of a fat embolism." Her voice drifted away from the phone at the end, like she was falling backwards, away from the receiver.

"I'm sorry, what was that?" Brian asked. "A *fat* embolism?"

"Yes, well, my uncle, he broke his femur once, falling off of a ladder. It was a pretty bad break, too: the doctors weren't sure if they'd have to put a few pins in it to keep it together."

Brian could hear her swallow. "Basically, when you break a major bone, a piece of bone marrow fat can escape and float into the bloodstream. In extreme cases, it can kill you, but before that, there are all sorts of nasty symptoms. One day, my uncle had no idea who we were, started screaming just like we heard you doing, and well, I know you are alone here at night and pretty much trapped in bed." Brian blinked his eyes, his vision slowly adjusting to the darkness. "It's important to be a good neighbor," he heard Jade say finally.

Brian blinked again. He could make out the shape of his legs, useless tree trunks wrapped in white gauze under the blankets, his feet two pointy lumps a few inches from the edge of the mattress. "Thank you, Jade," he said finally. "I'm fine. Thank you for checking." He clicked the red END CALL icon without waiting for her to say goodbye.

Brian looked in the direction of the window next to the bed. A long sliver of brightness peeked out from the slits of pane visible on each side of the drawn shade. He heard the house quietly shudder as it settled and braced itself against the late February wind gusts. Snippets of the dream he'd experienced just moments earlier flashed in front of his eyes. There had been snow, he was certain of that: a lot of snow. He saw the side of a mountain; he had been sitting, no, *lying* on some sort of narrow plateau in the middle of nowhere. Bright, new snow covered everything in sight: it tickled the tops of the pine trees in the distance, it spread like warm butter across the empty foot or so of space in front of him. He could not see what was beyond the cliff's edge, but he had felt a sense of fear. Was that what had made him scream? *Something* had happened on that cliff...but what?

He couldn't remember. After the sudden wakes and the soaked sheets and the intermittent calls from Jade continued for a week straight, he made up his mind to hire a night nurse. If it was some sort of medical issue, a fatty embolism or whatever Jade had mentioned, there would be someone there to help him, and even if it weren't, at least he wouldn't have to lie in cold, wet sheets for hours until the day shift nurse arrived.

A reticent, pale young woman named Penelope began work two nights later. She asked Brian to call her Penny. Her smile was warm and her manner pleasant, but his nightmares remained.

Penny rubbed the cuticle bed of each individual finger and took a deep breath. Brian was an easy patient alright, but the nights were getting longer and longer. There were only so many episodes of *Law and Order* she could watch in one evening. Her patient subscribed to the maximum number of cable channels, and yet he only wanted to watch the same one, night after night. Once Brian was asleep, she could sneak away to his guest bedroom next door and take a long nap. The biggest advantage of taking care of a man with two broken legs was it was a near certainty he wouldn't be creeping over to assault her while she slept: he was pretty much cemented in place. Even with assistance, Brian had difficulty moving his awkward body. On the multiple instances when she had changed his sweat-soaked sheets, it took her nearly an hour to alternately roll and pull his torso over and away from her, though she had been getting better at it. He was cumbersome, but not impossible to adjust. Left to his own devices, however, he'd be trapped on the bed indefinitely.

When her eyes drifted from the television set back to her patient, she jumped to discover he had been staring at her. For how long, she didn't know. "Are you alright?" she asked him. "Do you need anything?"

He continued to look at her blankly for a long second, then he responded flatly, "Tell me a story about your other jobs, your other patients." He smiled at her. "You must have some creepy tales, working the graveyard shift and all. Though I expect they don't like you to use that term," he winked.

Penny snorted, then felt her cheeks flush; she smiled self-consciously. "Not particularly. You're my first overnight patient," she said. "I used to work days. 'Not a lot of things creeping around in the daylight."

They were both quiet for a moment. Then, Brian continued. "I used to be terribly afraid of the dark as child. My mum put a nightlight in the bathroom to placate me, but even then..." His voice drifted off, and he turned at looked at the television screen, lost in thought. "It's funny: I remember being fifteen and still needing that light. I had just read Stephen King's *The Shining*, and the woman in the bathtub, she scared the bejesus out of me. I could see the edge of our standing shower from my bed, you know, and something about the eerie glow of the nightlight on that frosted vinyl curtain...I don't know. It just made the whole thing worse. I didn't really grow out of it until I went away to school, and even then, I'd be up most of the night in the dorm anyway, studying or whatever. I never really slept in the dark until I got my own place. I don't know that I ever got used to it." He looked back at Penny, then nodded at the heavy black flashlight standing on his nightstand. "Silly, right?"

Penny looked down at her hands. It wasn't silly at all to her, but she wasn't about to share her personal issues with a patient. She couldn't tell him that it was the darkness that had pushed her to take the overnight shift in the first place. She didn't know how to explain that there were some things that nightlights and visiting nurses couldn't scare away.

The ritual happened every night, without fail.

It wasn't enough for Penny to check under the bed; she had to slowly open the closet door, push the cramped dresses and blouses aside, and peer cautiously around the back wall, aiming her flashlight at the corner. She'd mistake the indecipherable shadows of her dowdy clothing making odd shapes as monsters if she didn't look long and hard. He wasn't there. Next, she walked to the other side of her bed, the two feet of space where she had sandwiched her nightstand, and the yellow beam of light flickered along the wisps of dust on the hardwood floor. No one.

As an extra precaution, she lifted the bed skirt on this side of the mattress, squatted from a safe distance, and looked. The space appeared empty, but just as Penny clicked the switch to OFF, she swore she saw a flash of grey moving. She quickly slid the switch to ON and checked again. She bent forward and silently crept closer to the bed frame to investigate, all the while holding the light in front of her like an acolyte's offering. There it was: a scraggly pile of grey matter, ancient and crumpled, a mummified hand with its fingernails jammed into its palm. As she stared at it, trying to get a better look, it shook ever so slightly. Penny flinched, her hand lost its grip on the flashlight, sending its cheap plastic casing to the hard floor, and the illumination died with a sharp crack. Shrinking backward and half crab-walking back to the foot of the bed, she scrambled to her feet and once she was righted, grabbed the lamp from the nightstand, shucked the shade from its top, and pulled the light to the floor to shine the naked bulb under the bed. The grey hand was not a hand at all, but a clump of pet hair and dust bunny, and as Penny waved the light closer, its feathery ends waved in the resulting breeze.

She was alone, at least for that night, but she was certain he'd be back.

Six months earlier she had developed a terrible cough, one that kept her up for hours at night and prevented her from reaching deep sleep. Her throat felt like she had gargled glass, but much worse than the pain was the lethargy that resulted from her restlessness. As she lay in bed, tapping her phone screen to play along with a monotonous puzzle app in the hope of lulling her exhausted mind back to sleep, she could hear the far-away ticking of the battery-operated clock in the kitchen. The room was dark, and the brightness of her screen blinded Penny from seeing anything more than two feet in front of her.

She coughed into her shoulder, wincing as the hot sting seared her throat. Her eyes watered. *Tick-tick-tick*, cough. *Tick-tick*, cough. *Tick-tick-tick*—she sat up in bed, letting the glowing screen drop face-down into her lap. There was another sound, something under the ticking. She pawed her nightstand, trying to reach the switch on the small lamp, but in her frantic attempt to turn on the light, she knocked it out of her arm's reach. Cursing, she felt along her thighs for her phone.

Tick-tick-tick-tick...inhale, exhale. There it was again. This time, Penny was sure she had heard it. Under the metallic clicking of the clock was a warm sound, a heavy sound: the sound of someone breathing hard.

Penny pressed the HOME button on her phone and slid her finger up the screen to turn on her flashlight. Slowly, she aimed the beam at the wall closest to her, then tilted the screen sideways to scan the entire room. Shadows danced in the crude illumination, but Penny spotted no face, no hulking body, no ominous form lurking in her room. She held her breath. *Tick-tick-tick...* the clock continued on, relentless and unmoved by Penny's panic. She continued to hold her breath, convinced that if she could be as silent as death, she'd prove to herself that she'd been hearing things.

Her flashlight stopped on the open door to the hallway. The door was not flush to the wall behind it. In fact, it was pushed away from the wall about six inches, noticeably narrowing the doorway. Penny could see the dark outline of the arm to her heavy flannel bathrobe that hung behind the door. It was a thick robe, but the door was pushed forward much further than it should have been. Penny crouched forward, resting her weight on her left hand while keeping the phone's light steady in her right. She kept her eyes trained on the arm of the bathrobe, trying to convince herself that no, it hadn't just moved. No, it really was her bathrobe; it was definitely not the arm of a man-like creature standing just behind the door, waiting and watching her as she slept.

Inhale. Exhale.

The sound was coming from behind the door. She leaned further forward, trying to glean a better look at the silhouette. Slowly, she shifted her weight and slid sideways to position herself on the edge of the mattress. She was so close to the door, she could almost reach out and touch its knob. If she could leap from the bed in one swift movement, a one-two step on the balls of her feet, she could propel herself out of the bedroom before he could reach out from the shadows and snatch her back inside, pull her back behind the door with him.

With the preciseness of a predatory cat, Penny stretched her legs to touch the cold wood floor with her toes. Ever so slowly, she relaxed her feet to place her soles fully on the ground and concentrated her strength in her thighs and left arm. Taking a final deep breath, she pushed herself from the bed and dashed from the room, breaking into a full sprint as soon as she was upright. Just before she was out of reach of the bed, she felt the stroke of bony fingers caress her right shoulder; her whole body flinched, and she dropped her phone and heard it sail under the bed as she rushed down the hall toward the front room. She continued to run until she was out of the house and had climbed into her car, locked the doors, and curled up in the back seat.

Long after the sun had resumed its place in the sky, she returned to the house. Her phone had been placed face-up on the nightstand. The cover was cracked.

Brian snapped his fingers. "Earth to Penelope? Anyone home?"

She shook her head slightly and forced a smile on her face. "I'm so sorry—I got lost in thought for a bit there. Please forgive me," she said to her patient and rose to stretch her legs. "What do you say we play a board game? Some cards maybe? Enough of this television for now," she said, snatching the remote from its constant presence next to Brian's hip.

Brian grabbed for the controller at the same time, and the collision of their hands pushed the small box off the mattress and onto the floor. Penny crouched to retrieve it, her knees making dry cracking noises as she sunk into a squat and placed her hand on the bedspread to steady herself. Brian stared at her hand on the edge of the bed. *Snow, a plateau of snow.* He once again saw the side of the mountain from his dream. The snow had been everywhere, a carpet of white bunting rolled out along the cliff where he sat. It spread to the very edge of the cliff where...where the hand appeared. The image materialized, the rest of the nightmare finally clear. A gaunt, decomposing hand reaching up from below, stretching toward Brian, reaching to use his leg...for leverage? To pull itself up? No. Brian shivered and finally understood. The creature that belonged to the hand wasn't climbing onto the plateau: it was reaching to pull Brian down with it. In the final seconds before he had awoken screaming in his sweat-soaked bed, the monster had thrust itself over the rock face and onto Brian. The last image in his memory was of its ashen face, its wet, black eyes staring straight into his while the gaping maw of a mouth, awash with jagged yellow teeth, opened wide to attach itself to his flesh.

Brian placed his hand over Penny's and squeezed. "Could I have a glass of water, please? I feel a bit sick," he said. "Perhaps cards later, yeah?"

Penny stood up and placed the remote on the nightstand. "Of course. Give me a minute." She smoothed her pants and walked down the narrow hallway to the kitchen. She touched

the switch on the wall as she entered, and the room glowed
with light. The luminescence twinkled off of the stainless-steel
appliances, glass cabinet doors, and chrome hardware; it
danced along the immaculate marble countertops and over the
tops of the ivory silk accent curtains. Penny opened the door
above the wide double basin sink and removed a short tumbler.
It was Irish crystal, like all of Brian's drinkware. Penny had
learned early on that although her patient lived in a modest-
sized house, its furnishings were indicative of the upmost
affluence.

As she was filling the glass with water, a loud rapping
sounded from the door behind her. Without invitation, a tall
woman with long, dark hair opened the door a foot and stuck
her head inside. "Hi," she said, not venturing further from the
mudroom. "I'm Jade; I live next door. I'm sorry to barge in like
this..." She seemed to be waiting for Penny to coax her inside,
but Brian had made no mention of a friend nearby, and it
seemed inappropriate to allow a stranger into her client's home
without his permission.

"Do you mind if I check with Mr. Shea?" said Penny with as
much authority as she could muster. She cemented her feet in
place and kept her eyes focused on the woman. Her dead stare
seemed to communicate her uneasiness, as Jade pulled her head
back into the foyer and shut the door softly. "Of course," she
said as it closed. "I'll wait right here."

Penny wanted to lock the deadbolt before leaving the
kitchen, but the woman seemed harmless enough, so Penny
walked briskly down the hall to the bedroom. She found her
patient asleep, bright images from the television blinking
quietly like soft lightning flashes about the room. She left the
heavy glass of water on the nightstand next to the flashlight.

Returning to the kitchen, she glanced at her watch again.
Less than an hour had passed. More out of boredom than

anything else, she opened the kitchen door, a wide smile plastered across her face, and asked the woman to come inside.

Jade the neighbor was taller than Penny, but she was wearing platform boots that added at least three inches in height. Their soles must be made of rubber or some other soft material, Penny thought, as when the woman walked across the tile floor, she glided soundlessly, like a ghost. "Mr. Shea is asleep, but please, have a seat," Penny said, gesturing to the breakfast bar in the center of the room.

Jade climbed effortlessly onto the chair and rested her elbows on the marble top. "So, how is Brian doing? I've stopped over now and again, just to check on him. Poor guy: he's rather imprisoned here, isn't he? Like an animal in a hunter's trap," she said, a small laugh dancing in her throat.

"Yes, I suppose," said Penny. There was something about the woman's familiarity that made her nervous. "It's very kind of you to check on his welfare. You live next door, you say?"

Jade drummed her fingers on the countertop. "Yes, in the house right there." She gestured toward the far wall. There was no window in the vicinity, so when Penny turned to look in the indicated direction, she found herself staring at the refrigerator. "Brian gave us a bit of a scare early on: did he tell you?" Jade continued. "Frightful nightmares. Screamed like you wouldn't believe: my dad and I heard him all the way in our house, and with all of the windows closed!" She touched her lips lightly with the tip of her finger. "The sound scared me something awful, to be honest. I've had a few bad dreams myself after hearing those shrieks." She looked down at the rings adorning her fingers, then back up at Penny. "I don't scare easily...I'm a writer, actually. Jade Wren." She offered her hand to the nurse, and Penny shook it but said nothing. Jade continued as if she had. "Mostly horror. Fiction. A few commissioned research pieces here and there, just to pay the bills, but I like writing the dark stuff, really." She paused. "But Brian's screeching: it was visceral, you know?"

Penny smiled, unsure of what to say. She didn't want to breach patient confidentiality, and the woman's intentions were unclear. Jade didn't seem to be in any hurry to complete her business and leave. "I apologize that Mr. Shea is unavailable. Perhaps you could try back in the morning?" she asked, hoping to guide the woman along her way. At the same time, though, she was slightly pleased for the fresh company, so when Jade began to slide sideways from the chair and walked back toward the door, Penny felt a pang of regret at not having cultivated the conversation further.

"No worries," said Jade. "If he wakes up, let him know I stopped by." She waved slightly with her right hand, then pulled the door open and disappeared behind it.

Alone again, Penny walked to the door and ceremoniously turned the deadbolt. She hadn't remembered leaving it unlocked after she arrived—Brian had given her a key on the day she was hired—but it must have slipped her mind. She checked on her patient; he was still sleeping, quietly snoring with his mouth slightly agape, and she soundlessly clicked the button on the remote control to turn off the television.

She had nothing to occupy her time until Brian needed her again, and it was too early for her to nap in the guest room, so she took out her phone and typed *Jade Wren* into the internet search bar. Multiple images of young women, most of them making those duck faces that always irritated Penny, lined up in her search results, followed by a Whitepages directory page, a Facebook link, a LinkedIn profile, and a strange YouTube video of a blonde child lip-synching to a 1980s pop single in German. She clicked on each of these pages but did not find the neighbor.

She changed her search to *Jade Wren horror* and was more successful. On an online retailer's page of Jade's books, she flipped through excerpts from an encyclopedia-like book of fables and legends Wren had titled *The Things that Go Bump in the Night*. When she landed on one entry in particular, she stopped to read the summary.

... From the folklore of North American indigenous tribes comes the tale of the wendigo, a creature that appears human and, like the Eastern European vampire, feeds on its victims in order to sustain its existence. Also like the vampire, the wendigo is simultaneously dead and alive, its skin decayed and rotting while its human drives—specifically, hunger—endure. The wendigo may enchant and then control a human being only to transform the victim into a wendigo as well, or it may employ its target as a procurer of further victims. As the monster consumes its prey, it grows in size; however, as it is never satiated, the growth is only temporary, driving the wendigo to constantly seek out additional meals.

Penny smiled. Jade, for all of her unabashed aggression and self-confidence, had left out a very important part about the Algonquin legend: the story was thought to be an allegory for an unending desire for wealth.

Out of the corner of her eye, Penny saw a grey shape sail down the hallway. She turned toward it quickly, but it disappeared. *A figment of my imagination*, she thought. *That's all it is.* She laughed to herself and placed her cell phone in her back pocket, then thought better of it, remembering the smashed cover months earlier. She placed the phone delicately on the countertop and walked cautiously down the hallway toward Brian's bedroom.

Her patient was awake but groggy. He blinked at Penny. His body trembled a bit, and his eyes grew wide. "What time is it?" he asked quickly.

Penny looked at her watch. "Almost eight. Still early. Are you hungry?" She glanced at the glass on the nightstand; all of the ice had melted. "More water?"

Brain's eyes darted about the room. In the dead quiet, the house creaked and shivered. "It's so quiet in the winter," Brian finally said. "All that snow. Too quiet, I think. Don't you agree?"

Penny sat on the edge of the bed and placed her hand on her patient's arm. They were both still, and then flinched simultaneously. Under the sound of the floorboards and baseboards and pipes readjusting, there was another noise. It was subtle, and when Brian looked to the nurse to see if she, too, had heard it, he was disquieted to find her countenance empty.

Inhale. Exhale.

Brian's eyes darted about the room, then he motioned with his head toward the closet. "It's in there," he whispered, his eyes wide and his expression feverish. "There's someone in the closet."

Penny scanned his face. He reminded her of her brother when he was a boy. He, too, had night terrors, and their mother worked second shift, so while on babysitting duty, she'd often encounter his fearful cries just when she herself was drifting off to dreamland. Each time he'd awaken, Penny would stroke her brother's forehead and try to soothe him back to sleep, but for what seemed like an hour, his pupils stayed wide as saucers: a tiny boy on a terrifying acid trip. The scariest part for Penny, though, was what her brother would say, over and over. He insisted to Penny that the monsters of his nightmares were real.

"It's okay, Brian," Penny said. She rubbed his forearm slowly, up and down. "It was a nightmare. Here: drink some water." She brought the glass to his lips, but he shooed it away.

"It wasn't a fucking nightmare," he replied. Penny could see the beads of sweat pooling in the folds on his forehead. "There's someone in the closet. Stop patronizing me and get a weapon." He frowned at her, snatched the flashlight from his nightstand, and nodded twice at the closet door. His voice now a whisper, he added, "Quick: there's a baton under the bed, near the headboard on this side."

Penny frowned. "A baton?"

"Yes, yes, a policeman's baton," said Brian quickly. "My father was a cop, and after he retired, my mom used to keep it in her car...in case of emergencies."

Penny knelt down, her bony knees pressing into the hard wood floorboards. She leaned her head under the box spring and looked.

"Just grab it, okay?" Brian called frantically. "It's right there, under the bed. Grab it."

Penny continued to look under the bed, saying nothing.

Brian tried to pull himself toward the edge of the bed. He managed to lean over far enough so that he could see the back of Penny's head. Her face was hidden by the bed linens. "What's taking you so long?"

Finally, Penny reemerged clutching a black wooden bat about a foot in length with a short handle at a right angle to its base. She pushed herself up to a standing position once more and walked slowly but firmly toward the closet. Clenching the base of the bat with her right hand, she placed her left hand on the doorknob. After taking a long and deep breath, Penny turned the knob clockwise and flung the door open wide.

Behind her, Brian shined his flashlight into the recesses of the walk-in closet. There was no one. Penny inched her way into the storage space, pushing suit jackets and dress shirts aside with the tip of her baton. Still nothing. Penny exited the closet and shut the door tightly behind her. She placed her hands on her hips and stared at her patient.

"I need you to lie back down and relax, okay?" she said softly. "I will put the TV back on and set the sleep timer."

"You heard it breathing just as I did," Brian insisted. "You know something was here."

Penny exhaled audibly. "I know no such thing. You had a terrible dream, and it colored your perception. I know it seemed real, but we talked about this: that's what night terrors are. You hired me to get you through them." She pressed her open palm against the sheet near his back. It didn't feel damp. "Would you like me to change the sheets?"

Her patient scowled and looked away, toward the blank television screen. "No. Thank you," he said curtly. He picked up the remote from the nightstand and tapped the ON button.

Penny sat on the edge of the bed and placed her hand on Brian's forehead. She stroked his hair back gently, like a lover, and after a long moment, he closed his eyes. Disjointed pieces of dialogue from a 1990s sitcom drifted from the television speakers.

Penny waited. She methodically counted to twenty in her head and slowed her own excited breathing. She walked carefully around the bed, pulling out the tuck of the bottom sheet with her hand. When she had freed the sheet from its tethers, she returned to where she had been standing when they heard the breathing noise.

Then, without batting an eyelash, she grasped the bottom sheet with both hands and pulled it violently towards her, bringing her patient toward the edge of the mattress. She let go of the sheet, grabbed Brian's forearm and thigh, and rolled his body as hard as she could, sending him toppling onto the hard floor.

Stunned, Brian looked up at her. "Penny? What are you doing? Help m—"

Before he could complete his sentence, Penny shoved the patient halfway under the bed. She watched as the thin, grey claw of a hand reached out from under the bed and wrapped its long, pointed fingers around Brian's upper arm.

As Brian began to scream, the creature yanked its prey closer to its waiting mouth and began to feed. Penny smiled. Perhaps she would request a day shift for her next rotation. At least for a little while, she was safe from the darkness.

Saltwater Fish Tank

NICK MANZOLILLO

"I want it," Billy Tanner said, his face lit up by the blue glow of the aquarium tank. The creature within was without label. It was loose-limbed like an octopus and more crimson than fire coral. It was long, like a barracuda, yet there was a thickness to it, with three fins that would flow and glide through the water like a piece of ribbon. Its eyes were composed of black little dots along an indented face that lacked the crease of a mouth or beak. Despite its long body, its three fins brought to mind the triangular upper half of a starfish. The thing in the tank was a Frankenstein mess that could easily have been doodled in a fourth-grade art class. Billy pressed his face against the glass and, a little louder this time, said, "I want it."

Billy's father, Mr. Benjamin Tanner, looked up from his phone. "Oh yeah?" he grinned, even though he heard the kid the first time. He admired his son for not asking. Leaders tell you what they want, plain and simple. "How do you plan on earning it?" Mr. Tanner asked. The art of bargaining, he figured, even an eight-year-old could learn that.

"I'll help the maid work."

"How about you don't get in the maid's way, like the big stink you made on Sunday, and we'll call it a deal?"

"Deal," Billy said, his breath fogging across the glass. They were no longer in the official exhibition hall of *Fins and Friends: Marine Aquarium* but Mr. Tanner had never been one for staying behind the lines, especially in his later years. There comes a certain point where everybody in Chicago knows your family name, your associates and your net worth, and, they don't just hold the door open for you, they tear down the walls. When Mr. Tanner was with his son, they could go anywhere the little guy pleased.

"Backstage" at *Fins and Friends* was a little like exploring the unused props section in the basement of a Broadway production. Empty tanks and heaving bags of fish food were scattered aimlessly beside banners and cardboard cutouts of dolphins and penguins standing upright in bathing suits and sunglasses. Backstage, biologists conducted their experiments and tended to all the sick animals in rehabilitation. It was also where the beasts that hadn't been found a place among the public displays were kept.

Mr. Tanner knew Mark Bridgett, the director of programs, because Mr. Tanner was one of the original investors. Shedd Aquarium was a popular tourist destination in the Chicago area, but *Fins and Friends* eventually become a steady enough competitor that featured live concerts, carnivals and other monthly promotional events that turned an easy profit. Mr. Tanner also knew of some "shifty" things that Mark Bridgett allowed to go on behind closed doors. To sum it up, you wouldn't believe the amount of hoops young, eager-to-learn marine biologists have to jump through. At *Fins and Friends*, if you were rich and smart enough, then during after-hours, your research knew no limits short of your own potential. Mr. Tanner was a gentleman enough that he didn't have to make any threats. While Billy stared at his newfound pet, Mr. Tanner waved Mark over from where he was talking to a fish-goo covered employee. He asked Mark for a number and then smiled at the lack of zeroes he was told in response.

It was a day and a half before Billy's new pet, which he was planning on calling Slinko, was set to arrive. He could hardly stand to sit and wait in front of his videogame consoles or do laps in his child-sized castle fort that took up half his playroom. It was summertime, but with his parents often working and his "play nurse" only being available during the weekends, he could find little to entertain himself. The several bags of generic fish food (in the form of protein pellets) that Mr. Bridgett sent Billy's dad arrived within hours after they left the aquarium, but apparently there were certain "procedures" that needed to be put in check before Slinko could arrive. Slinko was apparently so special and unique that Mr. Bridgett cautioned Billy and his dad to "monitor" the creature's feeding habits because he wasn't entirely sure of any dietary restrictions or necessities it might have needed.

That first night between picking out his pet and waiting for its arrival, Billy dreamed of picking Slinko up out of his tank and bringing the strange, slippery creature to the top of his play castle. Billy sang to Slinko about having to defend the castle from "bad guys, zombies, and Orcs!" In his dream, Billy decided that Slinko looked a little like a dragon, as well as a great many other things, so he placed Slinko on the edge of the flagpole at the play castle's highest peak. Deciding he wanted to snap a picture with his Xbox Kinect camera, Billy bounced down the castle's slide, but when he got to the bottom and gazed up at Slinko, he saw something strange. Slinko was gone, and there was another boy, sitting at the play castle's highest peak. A boy with blood red hair and black little dots scattered like bizarre freckles across his face.

"Who are you?" Billy asked the other boy, who opened his mouth and let loose a long *gurgle* that ended with him drooling out a cup's worth of yellowish liquid all over the side of the castle.

"Hey! Why are you sick?" Billy asked, but the other boy only gurgled louder. The bloody red hair turned golden blonde, just like Billy's. The black freckles faded like anti-scars as the other boy's skin became fairer, just like Billy's. Finally, the boy's face seemed to droop and sag as the cheekbones rearranged themselves and...he became a mirror. A mirror that continued to drool yellow slime and gurgle like a frog with a hook in its belly without an ounce of air in its lungs to even make a hearty croak.

"That's gross! You're weird! Get off my castle!" Billy woke up screaming in his sports car framed bed. Of course, his parents didn't hear him. Before his beating heart could steady enough for him to fall back asleep, he was overcome by the inexplicable stench of low tide.

Not even four hours after Slinko arrived, Billy was bored, playing the first-person shooter *Destiny* on one of his PS4s. His fingers rotated over the joystick lazily as he blasted aliens while Slinko, ignored, floated silently. The tank was a rectangular display case on top of a marble column that could just as easily hold a statue or some other inanimate object. Billy thought Slinko was cool and all, if only because of how weird he looked. Billy knew that he couldn't actually play with him in his castle like he did in his dream, or for that matter do much of anything with Slinko, but none of Billy's friends had a pet like Slinko, so that counted for something.

Billy began remembering the weirdness of his dream when he glanced at Mr. Slinko's cage and noticed that something was wrong. Slinko's eyes had changed, and Billy's stomach started to feel weird when he realized those eyes totally looked like a person's or that of some kind of land creature. Each eyeball was composed of a silvery blue iris encircled by white. The pupil was still a petty little inkblot. Slinko had no eyelids and seemed incapable of blinking, as Billy held a staring contest with it until his eyes began to water. Slinko's eyes lacked any kind of intelligence or even life, it was almost as if they were painted on. If it weren't for how those eyes seemed to shine with the same slimy texture as the rest of its body, Billy would have been sure of that. When Billy opened his eyes there was a silence that he could almost feel, and then Slinko blinked, mimicking him as its eyes sunk and disappeared into the hidden folds of its head.

"Holy crap!" Billy yelled, and his first instinct was to run out of the room to find his dad, or his mom, if she was home yet. Slinko stopped Billy in his tracks by humming.

A metallic echo, like a quarter spinning and circling down a drain began to warble from the thing that was beginning to seem less and less like a fish. It was as if the glass and water weren't even there as the humming grew louder and drowned out the music from Billy's still active videogame session. The creature's eyes seemed to grow wider as its body begins to tremble and pull itself together, tighter, like an orb. A black slit appeared below its humanoid eyes...a smile, the semblance of lips, and then white squares of bone began to pry that mouth apart. Teeth, the fish was growing teeth, just like Billy's.

Crawling on his hands and knees, Billy pressed his face to the glass. He'd heard somewhere that octopi can change their color, and of course he'd heard of puffer fish that contract and expand their belly's full of venomous spines when they feel threatened. Billy's nose touched the glass as the creature squirmed away. One of its fins began to stretch to the aquarium's lid, the appendage growing longer and narrower, like a tentacle without suction cups. Curious, Billy sprang up and removed the lid, wondering just how smart Slinko really was. He'd never heard of a sea creature escaping its cage before. Billy leaned the tank's lid against the side of the marble column. When he glanced back to the water, a toddler's red, sinewy hand extended from Slinko and grabbed him by the jaw. He managed to let loose a gurgled scream when his face touched the water. The sound of his voice barely rose above the tune of Slinko's humming.

When Mr. Tanner fetched the leftover steak out of the fridge, he realized Billy had stopped talking to the fish. "Slinko," he called it, like he never evolved from being a toddler. Still, Mr. Tanner wondered what his wife would think of the thing. It was beautiful in some ways, yes, sort of like a lava lamp or better yet, one of those jellyfish lava lamps he saw an intern prop on her desk one time. Mark was adamant that the new "fish" couldn't quite be classified, thought it seemed to like eating the generic fish food well enough. There was no guaranteeing how long the thing will live, but Mr. Tanner figured that if the worst were to happen then it'd be another educational lesson for Billy.

Still chewing his steak, Mr. Tanner walked over to Billy's closed playroom door. He could hear Billy playing his damn games again. Tanner had never touched those ridiculous TV toys, but he still knew there was no way Billy was *learning* anything from them. They're books and movies without the lesson, the intellectual message. They were simulated sports that harmed Billy's body more than they nurtured it.

Mr. Tanner pressed his ear to the door. He could hear something else, a low rumble, almost like an amplified version of when you press your palm to your ear.

"What are you up to…" Mr. Tanner barged into the playroom and nearly gagged from the overwhelming stench. The meat went sour in his mouth, and he couldn't help himself as he vomited all over the carpet. The carpet that was already damp in the first place…. Mr. Tanner heard the bathtub turn on upstairs and that damn Billy, what did he do? The room, and the fish tank, were both empty, the water still clear and tinged blue by the decorative rocks along its bottom. Why the hell would Billy take Slinko out of its cage?

Something began to rustle from within Billy's play castle. "Hey, you in there?" Mr. Tanner called to Billy. Someone was in the bathroom, and Mr. Tanner wondered if his wife, Gwen, had snuck in. She'd been a moody thing for the past couple of months.

"Billy, come on out. What the hell did you do with your Slinko?" Mr. Tanner asked and got nothing back in response, only more rustling just beyond the main entrance to the play castle. The inside of the thing was no bigger than a teepee. "Do you hear me? Come on." Maybe Billy had his headphones in. Mr. Tanner knew that Billy was still too big for that damn castle and that if he didn't eventually get rid of it then it'd be the place where Billy would finger his first girl and crack open stolen beers. Men do shit out in the open, and dare to be judged, Mr. Tanner thought.

Leaning forward with a back that got tighter every year, Mr. Tanner slid open the plastic door panel. Inside was a pale boy. His body was crooked, as if all of his bones were jagged. His arms, legs and fingers were squiggles, and his bloody red hair seemed to ripple with the life of a sea anemone. The stench nestled away in the play castle was again overwhelming to the point that Mr. Tanner was forced to dry heave as a sharp bludgeon of pain hit him square in the stomach. Mr. Tanner had smelled plenty of rotting food in his time (his uncle was a butcher), but this was something else. There was an awkward sweetness to it that almost smelled good, like the hot sauce Mr. Tanner dumped into his burritos. The contradictions began to form a headache that threatened to claw through Mr. Tanner's skull. Half mad and writhing on the floor, Mr. Tanner could hardly raise a hand to ward off the crooked boy, as the squiggly creature from the sea descended upon him. Those crooked fingers weren't forged by crooked bones after all. They were of damp rubber that sifted into Mr. Tanner's nostrils and open throat like the all-seeing eyes of an endoscopy.

When Gwen got home from her impromptu trip to the doctor's office, she wasn't in the mood for anybody's problems except her own. Doctor Vinny saw her immediately because he still remembered what her parents did for his mother six years ago when the poor old lady had no place to live while Doctor Vinny was drowning in med school debt. Gwen's life is one built on power and the idea that, when you share just enough of it, you get friends that can make you accomplish anything. Friends that will give you *everything*. With that all being a fact, you'd think it'd have been easier for Gwen to re-up on Vicodin.

Doctor Vinny would have had to file her as a new patient and apparently "they," as in government people Gwen had no ties to, checked for doctors that pull that kind of scam with their friends. She figured, if only her husband would run for office and quit just taking the mayor out for drinks.

Stepping through the front door, Gwen barely had a chance to set down her purse before a low tide stink grated across her sinuses. At her family's beach house, she would often take one of the rowboats out from their private dock and on days after the full moon low tide, Gwen would dread stepping with her bare feet through the rotted, flopping creatures along the beach. Gwen dimly recalled hearing about Billy getting a special new fish that Ben described to her as "weird, but kind of fascinating, like the most mesmerizing parts of an octopus and seahorse."

There used to be a time when Gwen would wish her husband would spend more time with the family, especially when Billy was a nightmare of a baby and she had to hire not one but two nurses to look after him. After Ben began working part time and spending more days at home, Gwen found that she could barely function. If Ben started coming home at night and during his lunch breaks expecting to share a meal and spend "quality" time together, then that would mean Gwen would have to give up all of the little pleasures she'd become fond of. Her painting had to get put aside because she couldn't find any inspiration when that man was airing his thoughts out to her every twenty minutes. Coming home to that fishy stench without the mercy of opiates, she immediately began to make plans to go back to smoking weed like a teenager.

"What the hell's going on in my house?" Gwen asked as she slipped out of her jacket. Moving beyond the front hallway and into the living room, there was a squishing sound as her heel sunk into the carpet. "What the hell Ben!" There was no keeping it in. The smell was neutral, coming from every corner of the apartment. How could one fish even do that? Gwen decided that if her bedroom smelled just as bad as the living room, she'd get a suite at the closest Marriot. Either way, that began to seem like not such a bad idea.

A banging sound began coming from the bathroom upstairs. Gwen could hear Billy's videogames in his playroom but Ben, he had some answering to do. She figured that he was probably cleaning the fish tank or something in the bathroom. A clear narrative began to form in Gwen's head. Someone was moving the fish tank around, probably to the kitchen and the sink, and it spilled all over the living room carpet. Gwen figured that maybe the new pet was in the bathtub, which didn't matter much to her considering it was the guest bathroom. Ben should've just hired somebody to do all the fish-related crap, but whatever happened was probably a part of his new bonding time with Billy. The man Gwen married used to be practical and efficient. He would've been the kind of father that led by example, that held an aura of tingling mystic that would've inspired Billy to fall in line and look up to him like some kind of legendary idol. If only Ben could see how his change of heart was messing up their family's internal balance.

With an arsenal of sharp words prepared to shame the two prominent members of the opposite sex in her life, Gwen burst into the guest bathroom. She didn't puke from the smell, but it pushed her back against a wall and forced her to squeeze her nose with two well-manicured fingertips. In the tub there was a boy, floating face down. Billy...Some primitive maternal instinct infected Gwen's mind like a parasite, as she ran and then nearly fell as she slid across damp bathroom tiles to the edge of the tub. On his own, Billy rolled over and sat up. He was in only his underwear and the water he'd been laying in was more mucus than H2O. It dripped off him in oozing trails of slime but Gwen quickly forgot the subtle grossness, as she got a good look at what had become of Billy's face. His eyes and nose were gone, and there was only a slack jawed mouth beneath a visor of beady black eyes. The back of Billy's skull was still covered in hair but it sagged, like the squishy pouched head of an octopus. A metallic hum began to emit from Billy's throat, as Gwen realized some of his teeth had fallen out. Her son or not, Gwen screamed and ran back downstairs.

She slipped again, on the soggy staircase, her clogs finding a stray trail of what may be the same mucus that the thing that used to be Billy was swimming in. Gwen's screams became short little yelps as she brushed through the living room and stopped cold when she heard sounds in the playroom. It was like the guttural choking of a man.

"Ben!" Gwen yelled and barged into Billy's former room. Atop a marble pillar there was a fish tank. Crammed inside was Mr. Tanner, his bones cracked, folded and bunched together like a pretzel. His skin was pale and peeling, his eyes blank, and white. A spindly, webbed hand grabbed the half-ajar side of Billy's play castle door and began to slide it open. The sudden rush of a strange, stomach-stabbing odor brought Gwen to her knees as she sobbed and puked, the dizziness immediate and pulsing through her veins. The stench of rot did nothing to describe the sheer wretchedness that filled Gwen's sense of smell. Her mind began threatening to tear itself in half.

What used to be Mr. Tanner crawled on all fours from the play castle. His hair was blood red, and his body was jagged and resembling a half-cooked ramen noodle. "Tummy," the caricature of Gwen's husband gurgled before letting loose the same soft humming Billy echoed upstairs. Gwen curled up on the soggy playroom carpet and stared at the dead thing in the fish tank. The name Slinko was emblazed on a golden nameplate slapped across the pillar. "In your tummy," the thing that wanted to be a person said, as the bastardization of Mr. Tanner crouched over Gwen and pressed both pairs of those rubbery appendages to Gwen's stomach. The fingers stretched, and spread, and Gwen could only tip her head back to shout as something crept down her throat. She glanced at the open playroom doorway and the last thing she saw was Billy, standing there, soggy yet solid, the back of his octopus head pulling itself together as his visor of little black eyes began to form a pair of almost human pupils. Gwen tried to laugh, as something else became one with her.

Mark Bridgett was the kind of guy that was always looking for a deal and when his good, if not sometimes distant buddy Benjamin Tanner offered him a bargain to buy out his aquarium, he took it. Transferring a business was always a pain in the ass, especially when *Fins and Friends* was meticulously set up to walk the fine line between an legal and illegal establishment. Benjamin cut him the check before even asking if Mark would part ways with the place. When Mark saw just how big the number was, he went along with the whole thing like the strange little blessing it was. With a pregnant wife ready to plop out another blond, spoiled child, Mark figured Mr. Tanner was rethinking all of his business decisions. All of that thinking must have started to wear away at the guy, because right before the deal he looked like he'd been cramped into a washing machine set on high spin.

Mark got all of his affairs in order in less than a month, and then the Tanner family became the proud owners of a new aquarium. Mark couldn't have cared less about why Mr. Tanner chose the aquarium of all places. If Mark were honest with himself, getting new animals had been proving to be sort of difficult. Forget whales, just maintaining the three dolphins the place had pushed him dangerously close to the over-budget mark.

A week after officially selling the place, Mark found out that Mr. Tanner fired every single employee. He even fired the marine biologists that were using the place as a researcher's paradise, and this, suddenly, began to seem like a big problem to Mark. If the wrong researcher started feeling burned, then Mark could still find himself in legal trouble. Hell, Mr. Tanner would, too. This is how Mark came to find himself standing outside the *Fins and Friends* management office, late one Tuesday afternoon, because some people, no matter how rich and powerful they were, just didn't get it.

Mr. Tanner didn't pick up his phone, but the lights were on, and Mark could have sworn he heard someone moving around right before he rang the buzzer. The management offices connected to the back of the aquarium. The whole place resembled a stadium because it actually used to be one for a city college before they got the budget to build a bigger facility elsewhere. Mark used one of the keys he kept to sneak inside, because at that point, both Mr. Tanner and he were in the same kind of shit, and so formalities could be cast aside for the moment.

The main offices were empty. As Mark headed across the main floor, he noticed that, while all the tanks and lights were on, all of the fish were missing...the big main tank that featured a spiraling observation deck that stretched three stories tall was completely empty, full of only foggy blue water. It had everything from sea turtles to moray eels, rays, and even nurse sharks. Mark heard footsteps and rustling, and the aquarium, as big as it could seem on a Saturday afternoon when it was full of screaming kids and frantic parents, was mostly a hollow place. After closing, you could literally hear all the fish bumping around the edges of their tanks. It was haunting, yet not unlike the pattering of rainfall on a bedroom window.

One of the backstage doors was cracked open, which was good because Mark had only kept a key to the main entrance. "Mr. Tanner?" Mark called, and walked in on a feast.

Dolphins and seals were sprawled about with their guts strewn across the floor and dangling from Billy's little pale hands. Mr. Tanner sat on a bloody, hollow turtle shell that resembled a throne, holding an angle fish to his face as he bit through scales and cold meat. Gwen was hunched over in the corner, surrounded by half-eaten sea creatures. Both Billy and Tanner were shirtless, with strange pot-bellies that, if Mark didn't know better, he would swear were full of babies. Gwen herself was bone-thin, and it seemed like she was starving, drained, despite all the half-eaten and still somewhat flopping beasts surrounding her.

"Mr. Bridgett!" Mr. Tanner dropped the angelfish and stood up on wobbly legs. It was as if he was made out of rubber: he stretched and lurched wildly out of proportion. "Welcome to the spawning!" A metallic humming began to emit from Mr. Tanner's slowly elongating jaw as Billy began to mimic the sound. Gwen moaned and shouted about "making it all stop!" Mark had seen all he had to by that point, and running away seemed like one hell of a great idea.

Of course, Mr. Tanner's long arms wrapped around the back of Mark's neck like twin eels the moment he came to a stop in front of the massive three-story tank. It's not that Mark forgot the horrors of that terrible feast, but rather, he stopped in his tracks because of the creatures fluttering through the murky tank's blue. Of the same breed as Billy's pet, there were at least two-dozen more Slinkos fluttering through the tank. When Mr. Tanner grabbed him, Mark was only able to pee his pants and regret ever accepting that weird, unclassifiable fish as payment from a fledgling researcher who was short on funds. That bargain Mark got really did turn out to be something else.

Valley of the Lost

CEDRIC GI BACON

Calamity Jane had fallen enough times to know that if she didn't act fast, she'd be a goner. And with the stinging arrows of the vengeful Sioux buzzing about her head, quick decisions had to be made. The blood in Jane's ears roared when it happened, when her horse's heel nicked the edge of a knoll and sent both rider and steed reeling. Thinking quick, she kept her limbs loose and had to consciously tell herself not to tense up and throw her arms out straight, lessening the possibility of broken bones and significant injuries. Jane then kicked free of the stirrups and leapt off the saddle, putting enough of a gap between the two of them so the equine would not land on her.

She bounced once, then tumbled to a slow roll onto her back. Everything went blue and black briefly, and she was unsure of everything for a while, with only one voice cutting through the haze.

"*Cut!*" cried director Cally Reynolds.

Shaking away the dust that had clouded her mind, as well as the Calamity Jane persona, actress June May rose shakily up from the ground and acknowledged the stream of blood which poured down the bridge of her nose and clouded her vision. The Sioux were a small team of extras, of which one was actually a Northern Paiute native named Talulah Jim. Dismounting from her own bay horse, her sun-baked brown features showed concern from underneath the veil of black hair, as she offered assistance to June.

"Are you alright, Ms. May?" the Paiute asked.

"Yeah, I'm fine," June said, checking herself. She breathed a sigh of relief, finding the usual scrapes and scratches, but no protruding bones. She wasn't aware of the gash across her forehead until Talulah ripped apart the edge her buckskin fringe dress and treated the wound.

"That should staunch the flow until the doctor sees you," Talulah said.

"Thanks," replied the actress, running her hand across the length of the makeshift bandage. It wouldn't disrupt shooting for long, with an injury such as this. She could easily cover it with her hat for most long shots and a few close-ups that didn't require any rough and tumble fighting. Which was, of course, to the relief of director Reynolds, who bounded up to where June sat. Next to him was June's costar, Chick Stone, who was portraying Deadwood marshal Wild Bill Hickok in the picture.

"That was a helluva jump!" he gushed, kneeling down and slapped the leading actress on her back. "How're you feeling?"

"Like I got hit by a milk truck," June replied.

"We probably can't use the shot, you know," Reynolds added, rubbing the back of his sunburnt neck. "But it'll make a great cut in the trailer."

"Great," June said sarcastically. She had grown used to having some of her more dangerous stunts end up on the cutting room floor. Morbidly she had considered asking for the cut frames so she could have a document of her near death experiences.

Accidents such as this weren't unusual when they made these *Calamity Jane* features for Republic Pictures. It was a low-budget film studio, and, when stacked against majors like MGM, Warners, or Fox, the company's cost cutting measures included a driving desire for ready-made locations in lieu of fully built sets. Here especially, in the desolate hills of Owens Valley—about three hundred miles north of Hollywood—

Republic could film all they wanted thanks to still standing homesteads and mining towns from a half-century ago.

Yet the grueling, assembly-line nature had left her somewhat bitter about the whole thing. It was as though she'd been doing these films from the beginning, and felt like the carrion formerly skulked and stalked, worn down, and eventually picked clean of life by those eaters of the dead. June was no more a daredevil adventurer than Doug Fairbanks was Zorro, and was aware that she and others were just all hat and no saddle.

Still, the thrill of having her name in marquee—even though "June May" was her studio imposed stage name, the producers thinking "Meyerowitz" sounded just a little too ethnic for a star-in-grooming—was a fair sight better than being stuck behind an operators desk for eight hours. And if she was really honest with herself, she enjoyed the admiration from housewives and daughters who saw her films, and believed in the heroic actions June portrayed as Calamity Jane.

It was just such a shame none of it was real.

Well, except for Talulah, who June saw walking her horse down the length back towards camp for water. The Paiute's heritage wasn't a stock character, and her dress not a costume, unlike June's. Yet for the purposes of the picture, it was apparently crucial to portray that heritage as an antagonizing force of destruction against the white Western hero. If Talulah felt a ways about it, she never let on, even as she was called back film after film to fill these roles. It was a living, intended to make June and the rest look tall in their saddles and imposing with their six-guns strapped in their hands. Whatever aspects of the Native American landscape were left, it was appropriated for the purposes of looking authentic where lack of verisimilitude appeared.

"So what the hell tripped you up anyway?" Chick said, going back down the path in the short, dry grass. The tall, rangy actor got low and examined the ground, then ran a palm along the earth. He stood, and removed his tall hat to scratch his brow. "Huh, well what do you know, you've stumbled on to something interesting here."

"What is it?" June asked.

Chick kicked up a layer of the earth with his booted toe. "See that? Sand and oyster shells there? My uncle once told me that when you've got this mixed in with the topsoil, you've got yourself a genuine Indian burial mound."

June looked back at the hillock. She had seen such mounds before, in Utah, Wyoming, and the Oklahoma territory, but never one so small and narrow like a mine shaft. She had a mind to call Talulah over to ask if she had an idea about it, but with the dying sun over their heads, it was time to pack up for the evening.

The sun had gone away beyond the hills in a long, dreamy summer twilight. The image created a cream-filled spectacle of whites upon pinks ringed with yellow. The ranch-style shack they'd found in Owens Valley was behind a corral, which housed their saddle horses, cows, and a pair of mules for the film crew's use. Everyone pitched in and cooked dinner and, afterwards, some of the cast would break up into smaller groups, cracking jokes and playing music, while others would mind themselves with card games.

June was finishing up a meal of dried meat, vegetable soup and cornbread, and was sitting with Chick and one of the grips when Chick became aware of Talulah approaching just out the edge of his sight. Out of costume, she was dressed now in a floral print shirt with a black singlet strapped over her left shoulder. The band around her head was beaded, and crafted from shells and abalone, along with a clove of holly affixed behind one ear.

"Say, Tally, wait a second," Chick said, catching the Paiute woman when she strolled by him, clearing her dishes. Chick helped her and placed them to the side. "Now, it ain't none of our business since we're just visitors, but I was wondering if you knew anything about that range of hills out there."

"There are many hills, Mr. Stone," Talulah answered.

"Yeah, we're surrounded by them. But I'm talking about this old Indian mound that's just up there a ways."

June watched Talulah stare at Chick long, before she finally replied: "It is not a good place. Best you finish your movie and forget that it was ever there."

"Kinda hard to forget about, 'specially since it knocked June here silly. Good thing she's got a hard head!"

But the Paiute did not laugh.

"It is not a good place, Mr. Stone," she repeated. "Let hidden things rest."

"What you getting at? You make it sound like that thing's ha'nted or something."

"Consider it for the best, for there are things hidden beneath the earth for a reason," Talulah explained. June knew a thing about that. She had learned, roaming the hills in Oklahoma, that there were many strange secrets in the mist-covered past.

Sometimes it was better to leave the dead alone, as it was not the living's place to disturb that which was lost for a specific reason.

"Come on, Tally, what's the big secret?" Chick continued. "I've busted into Indian mounds in Palo Alto and Baja. Hell, I figure the occupants been dead so long they don't care what we pillage. Hell, I've got a string of teeth from a Miwok warrior me and some boys dug up back in '23. Wanna see?"

Before Talulah could respond, Chick held the yellowing cuspids in front of her eyes. The Paiute turned and looked away.

"There have been more than just Paiute in this country," Talulah said, pushing his hand away. "My grandfather wove many tales of times strange, Mr. Stone, passed down from his grandfather, and his grandfather before him. Of things which my people saw unfold and of many wrong occurrences which happened long before your ancestors laid eyes on these lands."

"Yeah, yeah," Chick said dismissively. "I know all about the first white men round these parts. Francis Drake was the first Englishman, looting Spanish ships up and down the Baja coast some three-hundred and fifty years ago. I hear tell he passed along this spot back then."

"In 1579, yes," Talulah answered. "They camped not far from here, when he was forced inland due to a hurricane. My people were friendly with his, and they with us. We offered them food and shelter, and assisted in the repairs needed to sail with the next headwind. It was for their own good."

"And I bet where they camped, they dumped some of that gold in that mound yonder, right?" Chick said.

"There is no gold," the Paiute proclaimed in a low voice. "Drake's men bore only their arms, which was more valuable than any gold. When fighting their way through a land unknown, many faced a hard truth. And in realization of that truth, many others left their lives and their bones along the trail. What gold there was no longer remains in the mound, long dug up by hunters and prospectors."

June listened interested in this strange history of the Pacific Coast. Each state had its own myths and folklore, with many trails down in the Southeast allegedly being lined with the forgotten gold junkets of the Confederacy, or even the unaccounted for mines with untapped silver veins along the borders of Texas and Mexico, and rested in the banks of the Rio Grande. These were the mad dreams which lit fires in the minds of all who seek them, regardless of advice heeded to stay clear. June could see from the gleam of fortune which now rose in Chick's eyes and knew, having worked alongside him for four of these pictures, that he would do whatever it took to get into that mound.

Chick licked his lips and then said: "Well, I think sometime tonight I'm gonna dig into that old mound and see what's in there."

The statement caused Talulah to recoil in horror, and her dark brown features went ash gray.

"That would be unwise, Mr. Stone!" she cried out. "The curse! It will claim us all, my grandfather told me—"

She stopped short, then sunk into a sullen silence as she looked away.

"What else did he tell you?" asked Chick.

"I swore I would never tell," she muttered. "Each member of my tribe swore to never speak of it except to Paiute. It is a risk of such damnation to break that oath that one would sooner cut their own throat than speak the truth of that mound."

"So what's in there, Tally?" Chick asked again, growing impatient of the Native American superstitions. "If it's such a bad spot, why don't you tell me about it? Convince me why I should heed your warning."

"I am sorry, Mr. Stone, I have much to do," Talulah said abruptly. She gathered the dishes in her arms and scurried to the back, shoulders stooped and swaying with much effort. To June's eyes, it was as if a heavy burden had now been laid upon the Paiute, and the woman was not up for carrying it. She looked sharply back at Chick, who was chuckling while sipping on a cup of coffee.

"Why'd you go and upset her asking those kinds of questions?" June queried, once Chick sat back down. The actor was grinning from ear.

"Because I got what I wanted," he replied. "She knows more than she's telling, and I guessed right through her game. It's an Indian tomb alright, but damn it if she don't spin a tall tale. I'm sure her ancestors helped Drake bury his gold there, which is why she sworn to silence."

"I hope you're a better actor than you are acting like an explorer," quipped a voice. It was Reynolds, coming up behind June and Chick's backs. "Don't you do nothing to upset these folks. We got a sweet thing with them, and the studio don't need you lousing it all up going after fairy dust."

"Come on, Cally, think about it! We pull up Drake's gold, we can buy our own studio, and make our own pictures. We can make June here bigger than Garbo and Dietrich if we bust that mound open!"

The director licked his lips in thought, then shook his head.

"Nah, too risky. Drop it, Stone, and let's just keep on with what we've been doing."

"Alright, alright," Chick said, and June caught the humor in his voice. "I'll let it go. Sure would've been nice to be rich for once. What are you up to?"

"Me and a few of the boys are headed up into town for the night," Reynolds answered. "Been cooped up around her too long with you jokers, figure I'll spend a little for some R-n-R. We're taking two of the cars and be back after sun-up. You want to come Juney? I'm sure there's a fella down there who's a fan."

"I'll pass," June answered.

With the rest of the crew dispersing for bed, June rose towards her tent. But before she had walked away, Chick whispered, "Come on. We're gonna have an adventure when Reynolds and the rest leave."

"Are you insane?" June muttered.

"Sure I am. Insane for treasure. You know as well as I do you don't want to be working for a rinky dink for peanuts forever, do you?"

The speech from the Texan was like a bitter tree, producing fruits of common sense from its branches. The likelihood of being plucked from the obscurity of a Poverty Row outfit like Republic was low, and any career prospects past the *Jane* series just as dim. She didn't like going behind the advice from Talulah, however: the Paiute was always good company between takes, telling oral histories and even showing June some of her bead-making and basket-weaving techniques that were art forms in and of themselves. If the mound was to be avoided out of some sacred duty, then June believed the Paiute's instructions.

And yet, the life of an actor was a perilous one, rife with much financial uncertainties. June wasn't the first actress to portray Calamity Jane, and she had a suspicion that if she did not play ball and keep her head down, she would not be the last. After all, she herself had been only too willing to succeed the previous Jane actress; who's to say there wasn't another waiting on her to slip up?

She agreed, and well after everyone else had gone to bed, she and Chick took a pick and shovel from the back of Reynolds' truck, with June handling the coal-oil lantern to illuminate their way. Coming to the base of the hill, June swung its slight light at the heap of grass and brown earth which seemed to madden Chick's mind. He muttered about the virgin ore pulled up from forgotten mines, and minted coinage and doubloons lifted from Spanish ships.

What if it were possible, Chick had mused, that Drake and his men just fooled everyone into believing this was a burial mound, and told it that way to the Paiute to keep them from unearthing his treasure?

The tall Texan set to work, as it was not a light task: baked by hundreds of unrelenting noonday California suns, the soil had become as hard as iron, and mixed with the rocks and pebbles and shells was very close to impregnable for weaker hands. Sweat soaked Chick's pale blue shirt, yet he did not lighten his attack. Through his grunts and heaves, his effort upturned the earth around that mound with illusory ease; the fire of the frenzied hunter burned in every bone and thew of his body until he had cut through the tightly packed dirt.

"Eh? What's this?" he mumbled, bending low into the dirt. June swung the light so they could both get a better glimpse at his discovery. Several sprigs of dried holly were strewn about, along with traces of charcoal intermingled in the soil. June knew nothing about the holly, but had an understanding of the ancient people which reared these sorts of graves and the ongoing fires they would keep burning for days while they worked at their laborious task, with the evidence left behind just below the surface.

Chick knew this too, as he muttered, "Damn it all. Still though, there's got to be something worthwhile here. Why else would them Indians keep a secret?"

"Because it's none of our business," June answered. But the reply was drowned out by the pick striking heavy against something. She swung the light towards the object and saw a flash of Chick's grin. The object was a solid block of roughly made stone. Strange hieroglyphics unknown to either actor's knowledge were carved into its surface, and another sprig of mummified holly was affixed to the center. Chick brushed it away, and it fell to the dirt, crushed beneath his boot.

"I knew I'd find something!" Chick shouted in triumph. "Now all I got to do is find the soft point and wrench this loose. Something's got to be down in there!"

As she watched Chick nick and peck about the edges, June heard something like an uncomfortable crunch coming from within the burial chamber. This was followed by a faint rustling, and she told herself that it had to have been snakes. That it grew louder and volume, increasing in rapacity which matched Chick's, left her unsettled.

June's spine stiffened, and she looked to the center of the stone. She dared no further, and said, "I'll leave you the light, Chick, but I'm turning back."

"Spoilsport. You sound just like Tally."

"I can't help it if I avoid things I shouldn't be near. Maybe Talulah was right. I'm getting a strange feeling from this whole thing, and I think we should leave well enough alone, before it's too late."

"Where's your sense of adventure, Jane?" Chick argued, throwing out June's character name. "Supposed to be like this big bad heroine and you're afraid of some silly red man superstition about a clump of dirt. I'm part Indian myself, you know. This is like my own birthright. It's alright if I do this."

June shook her head, then bade Chick goodbye and hurried back down along the hillock. The cold dews of the night were slick beneath her sandaled feet, and she felt a certain bewitching movement sweep across the sand and grass. She halted when she came to a halfway point between the camp and the mound, and believed she heard something similar to a wail rise and fall with the tiles of the night.

The actress would have chanced a look back, and even walked back to the mound. But something halted her movements and urged her forward.

She chalked this up to exhaustion and possibly a light migraine from her earlier fall.

Sometime later that night, June lay in her tent when the lush comforts of sleep fell from her. She was aware of all around her, this strange and ancient land with its haunted hills and secrets. Horace Greeley had proclaimed for all to go west to seek their opportunities from an oppressive east, but what many found were not opportunities but rather death in many a strange form.

Those same specters of death loomed now, almost a hundred after the first migrations. Driving away many Native American tribes, those ranchers and homesteaders encountered the Unknown and Nameless in a strange land, ringed with the cold gloom of mystery. That they survived was a whim of circumstance, with the price paid particularly high among those settlers and tribes who warred over the land's ownership.

A waving sea of wind stalked the outside, bringing ripples along the cloth of her tent. And for a moment, June pondered the utter silence which now seemed to reign over the few members of the film crew slumbering. She prayed for the swift rise of the sun, with its life-giving heat and illumination over the landscape. In the light, the birds sang of hope; at night, there was nothing but the crack-kaw's of the vultures overhead, swooping low to claim the dead and dying. Just how many bones of settlers and tribal warriors lay in the dirt, picked clean by them and swept over by the winds of time brought a shudder to June's mind.

And then she pondered on that idiot, Chick. She shouldn't have been curious, as it was none of her concern if he wasted all that effort on nothing. Still, she couldn't shake the ominous impression those sounds left on her. If they were snakes, he should've been careful and left well enough alone. If they weren't, well, what else could even be alive in that mound?

Outside, she could hear shifting of the ground and much furtive breathing. A shadow cast by the moon loped around groggily, and trailed its hands against the fabric. June assumed that it had to have been Chick, playing a game with her and teasing her for being so scared of nothing. She thought if she ignored him, he might go away, but suddenly the tent shook, and June's anger flashed to quickness.

"Chick, if you don't leave me alone, I'm gonna buffalo you!" she cried out. The shaking ceased, but when she began to settle back into her slumber, a heavy object was hurled through the fabric, taking with it the foundational pikes, and the whole thing came down around her.

Dashing the ruined canopy from her head and crawling from underneath, June stood and looked around. Down the corner of the brush grown valley, she caught sight of a shadow moving with the glade. The moon had long set, yet the light was dim, and there were many things which could play tricks on one's eyes. But June, used to the sun and harsh winds of the wastelands during many shoots, recognized the size and shape of a two-legged creature disappearing over the horizon.

She called out, yet the shadow continued its retreat, going in the direction of the mound. Who did Chick think he was, throwing a rock through her tent? He could've varnished the ground with her brains!

"I'll fix him!" she growled, and went towards the truck, pulling out a small Flash Brownie movie camera and affixed a flash bulb into the base. She chuckled under her breath. Chick had probably thought by messing with her he could coax her back to the mound to razz her some more. Well, he'll get that chance—right before she'd shoot his face with a great ball of light!

She grabbed the spare lantern. She became aware of a peculiar trembling that had suddenly taken hold of her, as she regarded the gait of the dim shadow. It had moved at more of a slinking, unsure lope, unusual for Chick's long strides. Perhaps he was drunk, but, no matter; he'd rustled her, and she was going to get him good.

Upon reaching the slope of the mound, she lifted the lantern and peered into the darkness. Revealed to June were Chick's tools lying quiet on the ground, the lamp she'd left him which had now burnt out, and, where the great blocking stone had previously been, now a black aperture. The stone itself lay in the bottom of the excavations Chick had made, but she saw no sign of her co-star about the area.

Where he could've gotten to was a mystery. June had seen a shape move in this direction, that much was certain. He couldn't gone far and fast as he did without her overtaking him on the path. And yet, how could it move with such swiftness and disappear just as quickly made no sense?

As she meditated, she trained the lantern warily into the sepulcher. She was not certain what it was she feared looking inside, but she felt her comfort die inside of her when she saw the tips of Chick's boots first, then the edges of his jeans when she trailed upwards. Both were stained red: she recognized the dark, wide pool of blood the body laid in. Fighting back the urge to scream, she approached the body, trailing the light up and revealing devastating injuries that were done to it: great chunks of flesh were missing from the hind quarters and the chest, with one arm partially devoured as if by a bear.

When she arrived at the neck, she hesitated once more, spying the red ruin that trailed down his blue shirt. Raising the light further, June braced herself for that image of Chick's wide, dead eyes on her face, imitated so often in the movies they shot when the black-hatted villain died of his bullet wounds from a hero like Calamity Jane.

Instead, she saw nothing. For Chick Stone's neck ended at a raw, bleeding stump. It'd been ripped away as if it were an aging hickory tree refusing to yield to the song of hacksaws. Waves of nausea came across June, and she felt the faint aura of unconsciousness upon her. She remained upright and still, and backed slow away from Chick's headless corpse.

A faint hiss behind her back told the actress that she was no longer alone. Beneath the drunken glare of the moon's shadows, she could make out two tall, gaunt forms which had crept up behind her back. They were nude, and long, stringy red hair hung in front of their faces, while their long black fingernails dripped redly to the ground. A thud came, as one of them dropped something to the ground, and June did not have to train the lantern to see what it was, as the thing rolled like a bowling ball to her feet.

The severed head of Chick Stone stared up at June, though she knew there was no life behind those blank, deadened eyes. The sharp cheeks were shrunken, and the lips rolled back in abject horror, frozen at the sight of what he'd uncovered.

Then the two great forms were upon her, leaping with the spring of a panther. June herself rolled with the motion and, the Brownie in her hand, smashed it into the face of the nearest of her foes, the bulb going off and blinding the other. Dropping the lantern, she pushed her horror-racked brain to put distance between herself and these creatures, whatever they were. But the long, talon-like nails of one bit into her shoulder and pulled her down to the ground, and proceeded to tear at her face.

June writhed about, fending off the attack with one arm while scrambling across the ground for something to defend herself with. Her hand fell on the blade of Chick's pickaxe, and hope flared in her chest. Quickly gripping the shaft, she brought its blade deep into the face of her attacker, whose body jerked to the concussion and flew off her in a scream of agony and gushing blood.

Her brain reeled, but she had no moment for reflection as the other, recovered from his blindness, slid a long, cold arm underneath her shoulders and held her in a full-nelson. June raked and clutched at the stranger's flesh and came away with clumps of skin and meat in her hands. She then threw her body and attacker into the ground with a violent jerk, breaking the hold which would've broken her neck, sprang clear and went for the shovel in a volcanic push.

At the same moment the creature reeled up to his feet, she swung the spade, collapsing the face of the frightful enemy. Even through the handle she could feel the force cave the man's skull in like an eggshell, and she went for it again and again, every stroke reverberating down her arm. Yet the ruined face grinned up at her in frightful mockery.

Just as the monster prepared to advance, June forced herself to strike, finding within herself the savage need to survive. At the moment the creature leaped high, June swung the shovel's edge with as much fury as she could command at the neck of the monster. His body fell one way, while his head fell down deep into the gaping hole, coming to rest next to Chick's body.

The actress stared and breathed, and felt great tears of terror coming down her face. She questioned if everything was just a bad dream. It had to be, as there was no explanation for what had just come to pass. And yet deep inside her soul she knew it all to be true. June felt as though she had walked through a thick fog, passing from the rational world she known into something terrifyingly other and unknowable.

And then she heard the high, chaotic screams in the distance, which brought her brain back into kinetic focus. Lifting the pickaxe and gripping the handle between her hands like a battle-ax of old, she hit the flat mesquite and ran hard back towards the crew's campsite. She nerved herself for what she might come upon, the hideous medley of screams threatening to burst her ears the closer she approached.

The scene she came to caused the actress to freeze in a way she had not since seeing Lugosi perform *Dracula*: red, howling doom had fallen on the camp. Tall, pale, red-haired monsters similar to the ones she'd encountered at the mouth of the mound now rent asunder the tents, as the crew screamed through the pathways. Some defended themselves, using what tools they could lay their hands on, while others, reduced to gibbering idiots, babbled incoherently while the monsters swooped in and devoured them.

She saw a cameraman, gaunt and bloodstained, holding a pitchfork in his hands and sweeping at three of the creatures in great blows. None came to his aid, as the monsters leaped upon him like a famished pack of wolves, and June fought back the swirling sickness as she listened to the grisly sucking and tearing of bones and gristle.

Death stalked through the camp hideously, and June's brain could not shake the delirium which ravened through all her senses. She suddenly became aware of the horrors turning their attention away from the meal they'd made of the cameraman and onto her. Yawning gashes for mouths dripped red and slunk her way. The actress held the pickaxe high, knees knocking together, not knowing what her next actions would be.

Then a red mist flew in the air followed by brain matter to the ground, as one of the creatures fell down dead, soon followed by a second. The whirl of bullets had come from behind June's back, she turned quickly and saw Talulah Nightspring taking aim with a .30-.30 Winchester. When the monsters paused, the Paiute grabbed June's hand and shouted, "*Run!*" dashing with her to the shack. Bolting the door behind them, Talulah set to reloading her rifle, grimly muttering at the lack of ammunition they had, while June tried to push the dying screams out of her head.

"Do not worry, Ms. May. Soon they will come here and kill us too," the Paiute said somberly. Then, turning to face June, her eyes flashed with sadness that tore at the actress and she added: "I tried to warn you and Mr. Stone. But you chose not to listen."

"What are those things?" June cried out.

"The Paiute refer to them as the Old People," came the answer. "They are the original inhabitants of this land, with a name which the Paiute deemed appropriate for them and their dwelling."

"What was it?"

Before the reply could be uttered, the women's heads turned to a pounding against the window, and saw the burst of blood splash the glass. Talulah uttered instructions to hide under the table, when the long slither of a shadow slunk by, and they listened to the wet crunching which followed.

"They called it Lost Valley," the Paiute finally said in a hushed voice. "It is a place long accursed before man drew breath. Among the traditions of our people is the story of how

They would waylay Paiute, then kill and eat them, leaving remains for a feasting of the Morn. Beneath cairns and mounds around you will find the bones of many warriors who gave their lives to the fight, but one can only glut their soul with slaughter for so long. The Paiute spent decades in combat against them, before cornering them in a mound and placing the crimson inscriptions and wreaths of holly around, trapping the monsters."

"That's madness!" June gasped, then cupped her hands to her mouth. "There's no such things as undying monsters!"

Yet Talulah stared at the actress and said nothing for a long time.

Then, under her breath, she replied, "What is more make-believe, Ms. May? Pretending to be a cowboy superhero or Things from beyond the dawn of time, which now live and will kill again?"

June's answer came from the red madness of slaughter outside. There weren't many voices crying out now, she realized; only a few scattered moans from the dying, which would attract the Old People to where they were. Blood rained and spattered against the outside structure, as parts of bodies and shattered bones were thrown to the wall.

June felt her mind stagger and reel, and there was a very real thought in the actress' brain that she too would be killed and eaten. And that knowledge made her want to shriek, but she choked this back down.

"I'm so sorry," she whispered, and squeezed her eyes tight to suppress the flow of tears. "If I'd said something else to Chick, and told him—"

"It was I who should have said more," Talulah interrupted. She gripped the stock of that .30-.30 tight, her finger dancing around the trigger. The Paiute was not looking in June's direction, but rather at the falling shadows and black hands which trailed along the dirty glass of the shack. "I knew all about this part of the country, and the creek, and that mound of horrors. Yet I allowed my oath to give Mr. Stone his clearance to search where he should not have."

In the silence following, June May heard the staccato pounding of her own heart. The darting eyes of the Paiute gave her no ease to her shattered nerves, as she too gripped the haft of her pickaxe until her knuckles bled white. There was no time to doubt her sanity, or anything that was happening. It was real, in all its violent suddenness, and there were things that should not be clamoring for their blood and meat that were. Time seemed to pass all too slowly. Her brain was excited, her heart was aflutter with the danger. The wait itself, for a plan to form from either her imagination or that of the Paiute, was maddening.

Her body tense with the thoughts of a final death-struggle, she almost let loose a frightened yelp when Talulah began speaking.

"Dawn is approaching," the Paiute said, looking at a battered pocket watch.

"That means nothing," June quipped.

"It means that if we last these next few hours, the Old People will have to retreat, lest the rays of the day shatter them. Their only hovel is the mound which belched them forward."

June understood now. If they were not scented and discovered, then it was possible for them to run to the production truck and get far away from there.

Then a black thought swam across her mind.

"What of the town nearby? Or Cally Reynolds and the rest? Won't the monsters come back?"

"Yes," came the answer. "The Old People are roamers, and once they find this field has been tapped, they will move on to the next source for their meals."

The sweat froze on June's skin at those words. On what common plane could she ever encounter such horror, she knew not. This was no movie, and the monsters were not the stop-motion creatures used to fool the public. The monster would kill the public once they migrated south. Yet, seeded deep in her core, the actress realized that the hell unleashed needed to be tethered once more to save hundreds, if not thousands.

Abruptly, she slid from her and the Paiute's hiding spot and cautioned to the window. She stifled a choking cry of pain, at the hideousness on the other side of that plane of glass. Strewn about were the remains of friends and co-workers. The half-dried blood on her own face had grimed and clotted, but these hurts paled at what she imagined everyone out there had suffered. Arms and legs here, gashed torsos there, and smashed and collapsed skulls marked where they had come to die.

It was in this realm of the dead that the actress saw the grisly, red-haired monsters lumber; some were still gnawing on bits of bone and human beef, while others walked about with one focus on their minds. Gorged and sluggish from their red meat, yet still they continued in search of more. Silence soon brooded over the landscape, as the moon bathed the horizon with an eerie, milky glow.

Shifting her glances from the window, she looked around and took stock of their meager refuge. It was then that the faint glimmer of a plan began to form in her mind, when she spotted kerosene and coal oil lined up in the back.

It would be madness, what she was thinking, and there was no guarantee she would be successful. June turned to Talulah and said, "When Chick and I dug up the mound, there was a stone with a twig of holly attached to it."

"The holly in my culture represents courage and defense," Talulah answered. "We placed it on that cairn as a means of forever trapping the Old People so they would not rise again."

"Could even the tiniest sprig keep them contained?"

Talulah noticed the actress was eyeing the piece attached to her headband. She nodded. "Yes. We would need to contain them, however, and place the holly within so their captivity would be infinite."

"There's several sticks of dynamite in that production truck," June explained. "Blasting caps and detonators, enough to blow a hole for them monsters to fall into."

Talulah gazed broodingly from the actress and the wall, seeing past the walls of the shack and out at the Old People. She fingered her rifle, while deep thoughts knotted her brow.

"If you can give me some cover," June said, her voice wavering with the chokes of fear of anxiety, "I can run to the truck, grab the dynamite, lure them here, and set it off."

"It would be a suicide to attempt," the Paiute said. "But, there is an old saying, one not native to Paiute, that I feel is applicable in this situation."

"Which is?"

"Our time on this earth is a brief one, but brief though it be, one should make its brevity merry. I shall provide you cover, Ms. May, and pray that your plan succeeds."

June nodded and gulped. Wordlessly, she tightened her grip on the pickaxe and motioned to the door. The actress stood in front of that portal and breathed in and out, nostrils flaring. Scenes of similar last stands replayed through her mind, where she—as Calamity Jane—had to walk out against seemingly insurmountable odds. Out-manned, out-maneuvered, out-gunned, and outmatched; none of that mattered, at least in the construct of the movies. There would be that one little trick she could pull off that would turn the tides on her side, and she would win right before the big fade to black and THE END was plastered on screen.

There would be no luck of the draw, nor movie magic to help her now. It would be life or death, with the odds stacked against her.

Then June felt the calming hand of the Paiute, who nodded and cocked her rifle's lever mechanism, spending a cartridge.

June wound thin, quaking fingers around the knob and pushed, opening the two women into a nightmare, and ran into that hell without conscious thought.

Like black dogs of death, the heads of the Old People snapped up and reared in the direction of June and Talulah. And they came swarming at them in great hordes, while June ran into the melee. She let loose a scream that was drowned out by those of the monsters, their taloned hands close and clawing at her, tearing away her garments and gashing into her skin. But she continued on, racing and swinging her pickaxe at whatever came her way, the only thing within her sight being that truck.

With deadly precision, Talulah hurled bullets like stone from a catapult, and ran behind June's back to give her cover. How much ammunition the Paiute had left, June could not guess, in those fevered moments feeling the wet clips of the monsters' teeth graze her flesh. She saw their dark, empty sockets for eyes stare at her and reveal no empathy or emotion behind them, as she clubbed into their faces with her pick.

Silence came down around her like a sledge on anvil, and June's heart dropped when she jumped into the cab of the truck and scrambled into the driver's seat. Talulah had stopped shooting, and in that terrifying moment, the actress wondered if she had succumbed to the onslaught of the monsters. If she had, then she owed it to the Paiute to send these things back to hell where they crawled from.

Firing up the truck's engine, it surged forward in a sluggish motion before picking up steam. The Old People followed, clawing and tearing at the canopy and following the truck's movements towards the shack. June's vision blurred with the sweep of those hideous faces, and felt the crunch of skull beneath the tires.

She barreled into the shack, caving one side in, and scrambled for the box of explosives. The monsters tore at her and June threw the box into the middle of the floor, then grabbed a flint. The wave of Old People washed around her as the actress broke each jar of coal oil and threw the fluids about the ground at their feet. Striking flint and steel into a bundle of dried wood, it leaped into instant flame and trailed around like a great, crimson serpent. The intensity brought sweat to the surface of June's skin and the ash coated her sight. Yet the actress did not stop until, feeling great fatigue upon her person, she backed herself to a window and held her weapon and a blasting cap.

This was the end. She knew this. The monsters advanced with the care of a predator, flaccid lips sucking and licking in famished want. Some were burned and charred, while others shrieked and howled at their injuries. The scarlet snake of the flame had reached the dynamite, and reared as if to coil and writhe around it and swallow it whole.

The actress, disheveled and bloody, waited for the moment to come.

Then came a loud crash, as glass shattered around her head, and believing that one had escaped and gripped her from outside, pulling her through, June thrashed and kicked, until dizzying reason came into view and she realized it was Talulah, bleeding profusely from her head and neck, and running full-bore away from the structure.

Sparks flew around the shack, lighting the roof and a great score of flames preceded the fireball which engulfed the building. June squinted her eyes, looking at the leaping flames and hearing the bestial roars of the monsters break the chain of silence of the night. She closed her ears, shutting out their pleas to some nameless cosmic god of theirs for a salvation that would not come. A veil of red and black cloaked over all, as the two women watched the conflagration seemingly bring a cleansing to the area.

June's clothes hung in tatters about her body. Her limbs and breasts were deeply gashed and darkly bruised, but Talulah—who was just as worse—judged none of the wounds inflicted were mortal.

As the sun crept over the mountains and touched the red soaked plains, June gazed hungrily at the cleanliness of the dawn sky. Somewhere, far off into the distance, came the cry of an eagle and their long night's nightmare had finally scattered.

She and Talulah worked silently and quickly with the sun above their heads and the crumbling flames behind their backs. Using what they could of the ruined canopies, the women gathered the remains of their dead crew and placed them inside. The whir of vulture wings beat overhead, causing Talulah to scowl at the carrion eaters, until their grim task was completed.

Finally, they saved their final, onerous task for last. Approaching the smoldering shack, June watched as Talulah plucked from her head the sprig of holly. Then, without flinching or fear, drew a bead of blood from her finger and scrawled upon the charred wood the glyphs so similar to what June had seen on the stone Chick unearthed.

June hoped, for whatever eons a light shines upon the world, that the Old People would not rise from these ashes again. She fell back onto the ground and crushed her face into her fist, as Talulah sat next to her humming a Paiute prayer. Somewhere, June pondered, the warriors of the past were bestowing their pride on one of their own, for again pushing back against the monsters of darkness.

It was several hours later when three cars pulled up around the ruins. Cally Reynolds stepped out and looked around, lowering his sunglasses.

"Good lord," he said, looking from June, to Talulah, and back again. "Whatever the hell happened here, I hope *someone* got *something* on film!"

Lambskin

STEVE DILLON

We Never Close our Doors, the sign on the door made a false claim. Today, the double doors to *the Bank of Refuge* were closed and locked. *From the inside.*

Outside, a young woman peered through the smoked-glass windows, but couldn't see beyond her own reflection. She rarely could in fact. But today that reflection was made less solid by the fog of her breath. She wiped the glass, but only managed to smear her perfect image, making her reflection unrecognisable.

"Hurry up, Zilke, or we won't have time to get the rest of our costumes together," one of her companions complained.

There were several giveaway signs—a few clues, nothing more—that they were getting ready for a big night out. After all, Halloween was *their* time—it was when they came out to play, to be something more than just themselves. Sparkly, shiny props spilled over the tops of their shopping bags, and two of the group had already donned their 'Vampy Vamp' wigs and tiaras. The one who'd hurried Zilke, her lover Suzannah, was wearing fake, black hair. It was highly flammable, no doubt, and was puffed up high on her head with white zig-zags on each side in case people didn't get who she was supposed to be. Had she thought about it, even her best friends and her folks had never 'got' who she was supposed to be, just that she was never truly able to be herself. Weren't comfortable either with her choices or her innate feelings.

"Anyway, I saw that Oonagh Headley go in there," Suzannah spoke again, "and you don't want to be seen talking to her—she's right skanky, she is."

"I heard she's a furry," one of the other girls laughed. "You know, those weirdos who dress up as fluffy creatures so they can shag each other like animals!" This was Trudi, who'd only last night overshared with the others how she preferred it from behind. Not that there would be any accusation of hypocrisy from the others, as none of them would remember; it had been such a drunken night.

Zilke admired her reflection for a few moments more, content in the knowledge she had no need to dress up to get laid. She barely wore any makeup in fact, and when she wasn't banging Suzannah she had a list of men or women she could call upon for a shoulder to cry on, or a sympathy shag if it came to that. She checked the door for a sign which might indicate when the bank's doors might reopen but there was none. She even looked around to see if there were any other doors, and finding none, she shrugged, turned, and walked back to join her fellow fancy dressers.

She decided she could come back later if she couldn't get money from the olds.

Inside the bank, Oonagh Headley (skanky, she'd been called but fortunately hadn't overheard) was starting to sweat. Even though it was a late October afternoon—mid-autumn in Refuge—the bank's heating system was getting to her, and she was losing her patience. She recalled why she'd visited the bank on this sunny October afternoon.

She needed spendies to buy a bottle of something to help the night along—it's Halloween, after all, she smiled to herself. *My night!*

The stocking-faced men she'd mistaken earlier for fancy-dressers or student pranksters were getting on her tits.

If you're going to shoot someone, get on with it.

And with that thought—*Bang!*

The sound was deafening in the confined space of the bank's lobby. Following the bullet, the sound ricocheted off the ceiling and through a window, but some of it spilled out and settled in Oonagh's ears, creating a high pitched whine. She rolled her eyes to the ceiling when she saw the other hostages jumped.

Most of them had probably never heard a gun before, or seen blood flow either.

She tutted and let her eyes roam around the room. They halted on the idiot nearest the door, the one whose gun had gone off by accident.

He was looking in turn at the other three gunmen, shrugging his apology.

"Wot you go do that for, fuckwit?" nodded one of the stockings to the door man.

This one was watching the hostages, or supposed to be. He was sitting on the corner of a table, probably to get a wider view of the lobby. Oonagh reckoned she'd have him on the floor with his throat cut before he'd even noticed she'd moved. Except there were other people—innocents—in the room, and she daren't risk it.

For their sakes: not on her own.

"Man—I didn't mean to, it just went off, didn't it?" the door man offered by way of an excuse.

"More like you bottled it, dick-for-brains," replied the watcher. "Just cool it, yeah? We'll be out of here in no time now—as soon as these banker-wankers have got that safe open."

"Yeah, bruv. I'm cool," the doorman sniffed as if to prove his coolness.

But he wasn't, and Oonagh had his mark. He'd be the last to be taken down, and might even save his own life if he pissed himself and cried in the corner when the action started.

Sitting with her legs out straight, she cracked her fingers against the floor. The watcher swivelled on the corner of the table to face her.

"Wot you up to, tiny-tits? Got somewhere to go, 'av you?"

She shrugged and held out her hands, palms upward to show she wasn't trying to conceal anything.

While he was still eyeballing her, she shuffled her feet together like they were itchy, edging the dagger out of her sock just far enough so it couldn't be seen by the watcher.

"Sorry—nervous habit. I get eczema."

She kept talking, kept his eyes on her lips. Mundane drivel about her ma and the doctors, and how nothing worked to stop the itching.

This is the magician's secret—to hide in plain sight and distract the watcher.

She was cocky, sure, but she knew she was good.

As soon as the blue lights started flashing, Oonagh would make her move, and she decided now he'd be the first casualty. She looked around, counting the heads on this side of the glass-partitioned counter, and strained to see the goon who was shoving the old bank-clerk around.

There were five norms squatting on the floor, plus the four stocking-heads, plus the teller.

Plus—herself, Oonagh...

Plus—the cute guy with a wolfish grin who was a little bit too old for her, but she blushed anyway when he caught her looking.

Being a hostage was exciting, brought a throbbing to her ears. *This was something to tell those stuck up bitches from school about.*

Although she hated coming into the docklands during daylight hours, there was no other way to get to her money. Not that she had much—working a stall in the market selling dodgy clothes and jewellery didn't exactly make a fortune. The most expensive piece of clothing she was wearing was a faux fur wolf-head hood. The leathers were fake, like the smile she wore all day at work.

She'd heard at school that in the digital age—before the big crash—people had automatons to get money from. *Holes in the walls,* and you got your money by tapping in a secret code that only you knew. According to the few history books that still survived, it had been one of the triggers for the apocalypse. Before all the computer systems came to a crash, they called it *electronic banking.* It ended with what her teacher had called 'war by financial subterfuge'.

With hardly any computers—the big one at the *Refuge Reporter* was the only one Oonagh had heard of—everything was manual, and slow. But at least she got to meet people in here. People who treated her with respect, not trying to barter every last cent of profit out of her on the stalls. After banking here for so long, she even recognised the bank clerk. He was a kind man—*person*, she corrected herself—one of the Marsh-folk, and she hoped the goons with the guns wouldn't hurt him.

Zeév Şandru yawned and looked about the room, hugging his lambskin jacket for warmth. It wasn't quite up to Refuge's cold winds, but it was part of his uniform. The badge on his sleeve gave it away to anyone with eyes to see: a wolf's head, in a circle, its fangs bared. Two letters—WB—Wolf Brothers of course, and his number, which was 3.

That fucking idiot with the shaky trigger-finger would have to go first: he was dangerous, too risky. The other guard—the watcher—was a lot cooler, and he'd most likely down tools and lay on the floor when the change came over Zeév.

And the change would come—he wouldn't stop it this time. This time, the strength and power it brought might do some good for once.

He smiled at the young woman who was still eyeing him up. She was far too young for him, but he could see she was different. Besides the wolf-hood she was wearing—fake, but said a lot about her—Zeév was impressed by how she'd stealthily made her concealed dagger more accessible. She'd managed to keep it secret from the meat-bag who was sitting on the table, even while he was watching her intently.

Clever. Confident. He could do with her help. At least, he'd give her the pleasure of adding to the kill count if needed—he decided to leave the watcher for her to deal with.

The other hostages were all norms: Refugeans going about their daily business. The girl could obviously fend for herself, but with four goons, Zeév might still have to move fast to avoid any bloodshed from the innocents.

"What you gawkin' at? Who are you, anyway?" the watcher pointed his gun at Zeév.

"Not gawking—just taking it all in," he replied.

"And what you thinkin', Mister-taking-it-all-in?" the watcher snapped back.

"That...you seem to have everything under control—well-planned. But do you think the mayor will let you get away with...this?" He jutted his chin up and gazed around the room.

"You know; I don't like your manner. You're too cool. You think you've got a chance? Well, you 'aven't. Anyway, what makes you think the mayor doesn't want us to get away with all this?" He waved his gun hand around the room. "Besides, we have you and little miss tiny-tits here to give us some cover from the cops. Not that we'll need it, but it'll look good in the paper. Ahhh...the cops'll make out they're doin' what they can to stop us gettin' away, but the mayor's already sorted it. And we've got these..."

He pulled back his hood enough to reveal body armour under his heavy jacket.

Not cheap, Zeév thought. He must have inside connections, and if the mayor was involved...?

Zeév rocked his head back, closed his eyes and breathed deeply, then said between gritted teeth, "The mayor's behind this heist? Fuck, that's twisted!"

"Yeah. He's a smart cookie, knows how to get things done," the watcher grinned at Zeév. "But not quite as smart as we are."

He tapped the gun to his temple. "Soon as we get this little haul away from here, we're gonna use it to turn the tide against 'im and all 'is suits. That fucker's bad news for this town, but 'e's gonna get a whole lot more trouble for 'imself when we make it away with this little pile of dosh and use it against 'im!"

Zeév was open-mouthed. He'd really misjudged these stockings as small-fry opportunists and goons.

Plotting to rid Refuge of its corrupt mayor, they may actually be trying to do some good, in their own way.

On a different day, perhaps he might have joined with their anarchy—he'd certainly add a lot of muscle to their little revolution. But not today, not with all these norms at risk.

He rested his head against the wall and closed his eyes.

And waited.

Oonagh hated carrying ID; it stole away her right to anonymity. Prove you're who you say you are; prove this money is yours; prove your age; prove, prove, prove.

Even when she showed her ID, she was still looked at suspiciously—like she wasn't herself.

Anyway, why couldn't a young Refugean have an income and a bank account? Why did everyone assume she was a scammer or a dealer? Except here. At this bank, Ezekiel—the bank clerk—smiled at her and was always polite, friendly. For an old dude in Refuge, that made a nice change, and was the main reason she banked here instead of the council-run Refuge City Bank.

She could just be herself here, even though sometimes she felt the need to pretend in order to fit in. In fact, when she'd first arrived at Refuge, she'd told her school-friends she'd smuggled a small fortune past the robbing bastards at border patrol.

She'd been lucky to survive the 'quake that demolished her own town—that much was true. But that was everyone else's story. So, amid the chaos, she told her friends, she got smart quickly. After the briefest period of mourning for her family, she told them how she'd hopped from house to house, grabbing all the cash, jewellery, and gold she could find. She'd elaborated when her friends' eyes widened. Told how she'd coolly slipped her way past Refuge's dockland security with tons of goodies in a sparkly girly-bag.

Well, what was left of it, she said, laying down another lie. It had cost her a tidy sum to bribe her way to Refuge, she claimed. Thankfully, the mayor had a 'back-door' policy for the rich; everyone knew that. But, she'd continued, it had cost a whole lot more than that to avoid spending her first night in Refuge at the Temple of Bes. Whoring herself for the pleasure of the mayor's men was something she'd never, ever do—sadly that was another lie.

To prove the lies, Oonagh had offered to buy stuff for her friends, would take them all to Refuge's Beast Market to get them costumes for the fancy dress party.

The reality was much different. Oonagh had escaped by boat, like many before her. She'd arrived in poverty, like the others. She'd been abused—unsurprisingly—then when the newness of this latest arrival had gone, she'd been let loose from the Temple of Bes and kicked out onto Refuge's streets where she'd stolen food, essentials, and vintage clothes purloined from the stalls in the Beast Market. Eventually she was caught, of course, but some kindness had been shown to her by the owner of a stall, who gave her a job, under her own watchful eye, naturally.

It hadn't taken her friends long to figure out the truth. Oonagh worked in the Beast Market, which was part of the Docklands, within the town's walls, but she actually lived outside the town walls. That was a big deal, and her friends laughed when they learned that.

She'd made home somewhere deep in The Maze, which—according to *The Refuge Reporter*—was a seedy den of thieves just outside the boundary. Surrounded by Refuge's poorest—immigrants like her who couldn't afford to live within the city walls—she had a job at least, so she helped others out when she could: little food and hygiene packages left for the homeless, shampoos and soaps, some stolen toys for the poorer children.

When she wasn't working, she slept in a dive by day, enjoyed the street life by night. Kept to herself now she'd been tagged by her old friends as 'a skanky liar'.

The way Oonagh took it, she was a liar out of necessity. She despised her real name, the one on her ID cards—*Destiny*. Despised too how she'd grown to look so much like her mother. It was too painful, carrying a photograph everywhere she went, pretending to be normal, when in fact she knew she was special: Deep within her, she was a shadow; a stealthy assassin—a *nobody*, which made her *somebody*. All this ID nonsense went against her natural urges to stay hidden, cling to the shadows, not get picked out or picked on.

Oonagh looked around the room at the other hostages, glad she was still free, enjoying herself even, amused that the loonies who were trying to raid the joint couldn't see how much she was enjoying the adventure.

"Toima! What the fuck is holdin' you up—get that fucking safe open will you?"

The watcher was still sitting on the table, swinging his legs as he shouted. Toima knew the drill all right: he'd been on many operations like this in the old country: *Get the job done, get out. Kill if you need to, but not if it slows you down.*

"It's this fucking ugly banker, Jonah—he's shitting himself with fright. He's fumbling the keys on me."

"You need me to come and do the man's work, Toima? Get a fucking move on!"

For all his pretence at coolness, Zeév was now sweating. He'd kept the beast at bay too long, waiting for the right moment, even thought about taking side with the stockings—help them get through this and out the other side safely.

But when the watcher had revealed their plans, boasted about the mayor's involvement—and how they were going to betray the mayor, Emeritas—he knew then that the hostages were all going to end up dead, one way or another.

He'd be included in the slaughter if the stockinged goons had their way. Along with the girl with the dagger and the wolf-hood...

It wasn't something he'd let happen, even if he did sympathise with their cause. He despised the mayor and all he stood for, but this was wrong, not the way to go about things. He wished he hadn't been caught up in all this, wished he could just read about it in tomorrow's *Reporter* and perhaps cheer the robbers on for putting one over on the corrupt mayor.

"Are...are you quite sure you need everything in the safe?" Ezekiel adjusted his tinted glasses as he pleaded with the stockinged man called Toima.

"Everything. All the fucking cash and jewellery and other good stuff—anything these rich bastards have squirrelled away over the years. Keep nothing from me, or I *will* kill you."

"Everything?" the man gulped.

"All of it." Toima looked at the clerk's name badge. "Ezekiel. Good name. Reminds me of the olden days. So...yeah, everything. We're gonna come up against the fucking mayor with all we can—money, guns, cash, some of that precious

Marsh-people jewellery and shit—anything to help us kick him the fuck out of office."

Ezekiel gulped again. He fumbled, dropped the keys. He stooped awkwardly to retrieve them; neither his bloated body nor his webbed fingers were designed to be nimble. Finally, he managed to turn them in the lock, the door slowly swinging open and seeming to suck the sound out of the corridor behind them.

"It's all yours. Take everything. I'm sorry, so sorry—I need to go to the toilet. Now!"

"Oh, just fucking go and do what you have to, you old fart!"

"Got it open yet?" the watcher shouted.

"Just done it. I'm letting the old man go to the crapper before he shits on the floor."

Ezekiel shuffled past the door that led to the public area, to another marked 'Staff only'. He looked at the gunmen in turn, then nodded to the sign above the wooden door. It didn't show a man, or a woman, just a toilet. As nobody stopped him, he pushed the door open and locked himself inside.

The sound of sirens was the trigger. Nobody else in the room had picked up on it yet.

It's time.

Zeév dropped his head between his knees, slowed his pulse, filled his lungs, and unbuckled his belt. If he kept the leather belt on, it would hurt like fuck the day after the wolf was let loose. It would dig into his belly and leave a bloody crease that lasted a week.

He lifted his head to take another body count, conscious of the hairs that were already sprouting from the sides of his nose as his snout extended.

The claws felt good, itching to make their mark.

That girl had better be good with her knife if they were to stand a chance of taking out all the stockings before one of the norms got shot.

He looked at the watcher, to check he hadn't noticed the change taking place.

The watcher was distracted, had turned his head toward

Toima to see if he'd made progress with the safe.

Zeév slipped out of his lambskin jacket and kicked off his shoes. He smiled at the thought: it always tickled him and wondered why the norms hadn't yet sussed it—lambskin jacket: a wolf in sheep's clothing.

There was a huge splash from the toilet the bank clerk had locked himself in. Toima grinned at first, then looked concerned as the watcher glared at him. *The splash was too big,* he now realised. He banged on the door to get Ezekiel to open it up.

"You fuckin' idiot, Toima," yelled the watcher, "couldn't you see he's one of them Marsh people who run the other half of this fuckin' town? Probably jumped down a sewer and swam away!"

Toima stopped banging, rested his head on his arm and said "Fuck. Sorry, man. I didn't think. Just thought he needed the crapper."

Then the shit really hit the fan...

Flashing blue lights and wailing sirens filled the air.

The wolf stood from his crouched position, towering above the seated watcher in one swift movement. He turned and pounced, tearing out the doorman's throat out as he landed.

As the wolf turned again, the watcher dropped off the table and onto the floor.

The girl can see to him, the wolf thought.

It turned to the other stocking by the window and bounded across the lobby. It ripped through the man in a furry, bloody haze—amid sounds of snarling, screaming, and gurgling.

From the corner of its eye, the wolf saw the girl swivel her legs in the air and scissor-kick to her feet, stepping over to where the watcher lay hiding behind the table.

It left the girl to do what she'd been clearly itching to do: slice the throat of the watcher. It saw her take the knife from her sock and turned again. In one leap, the wolf bounded over the thick sheet of glass that reached from the counter almost to the ceiling, separating the bank tellers from the public area. The partition wasn't high enough, though. It was over in one standing jump. Then it took out the last of the stockings as he came running from the coffin-sized safe, waving his gun.

Job done. No innocent blood spilled.

Then it heard the gun shot, watched in horror as, apparently in slow motion, the girl was spun around by the impact, blood spurting from her chest. Her dagger was still in her hand as she fell.

The wolf bounded back over the glass partition into the lobby and bit off the watcher's hand taking the gun with it. As it ripped the stocking from the man's face and tore at the pulsing throat, it saw the girl's knife on the floor.

It was confused and distracted, and cocked its head to one side. It had seen the girl retrieve the knife, watched as she lunged toward the watcher. How could she have failed? She'd seemed so confident...

It sniffed at the knife—the plastic, replica knife. It was the kind sold in Refuge's Market stalls, along with the black Vampy Vamp wigs with white zig-zags—the kind bought by fancy dressers, Halloween party-goers, wannabe witches, ninjas and warriors.

And the ones who dream of being different.

The wolf nudged the dead girl's hand, then howled and bounded once more, crashing through the smoked-glass windows and away into the streets of Refuge, determined to hide the tears that rolled down its snout.

The Case of the Wizard-Cat, Who Wore a Rotted High Hat

KATE WATTS

I had recently suffered a debilitating brain fever—brought on, my physician declared, by an unwholesome dedication to my occult studies—and was convalescing in the home of my widowed mother. As she had traveled to Arkham for the day, I had hoped to entertain myself by netting a few rare butterflies in our garden, but the intermittent rain dripping from the ashen skies permitted no sun, and the chill air provoked in me a disagreeable ennui. My butterfly net therefore abandoned in the hallway, and I thus confined with only my pet turtledove, Clara, as company, I confess that a longing for my abandoned studies weighed upon me.

My mam had, however, obtained my promise of forbearance; thus, I resolved to settle by the roaring fire, a monograph on that infamous Bostonian painter Richard Upton Pickman in my lap, with afternoon tea laid out nearby and a delicate, Oriental fan at my side should I grow hot. The somewhat academic text, however, failed to wholly engage me, and I soon lost myself in brooding over the unnerving images of Pickman's painted nightmares.

Few scholars dare dispute that aught but Pickman's morbid

derangement conceived the anthropoid dog-things he had so
favored as subjects, but as I perused the slim volume, I recalled
fragments of a certain tale told of an ancient seafaring ancestor
of mine. His schooner heaving up on an unwholesome shore, he
discovered himself—so it was said—not among men, but rather
at the mercy of a pack of hideous fiends performing an
unhallowed rite. The exact nature of either the fiends or their
rites he refused to disclose, but as my poor relative quaked to
hear the howling of cats, it was suspected that the fiends of his
hallucination were to some degree catlike.

The incredible tale could not be real, of course, but raising
my gaze then to contemplate the reproduction of my ancestor's
very schooner, the *Emma*, which my mother displayed among
her most cherished curios, I soon fell to meditating upon my
kinsman's mad dream.

Perhaps I drowsed—indeed, sane men may dismiss my
account as the phantasy of my illness. But at some indistinct
time thereafter, my reverie was disturbed by an ominous
thump. I started to my feet, but discovering that only wan
embers remained of my fire, I concluded I had heard only a log
collapsing in the flames.

Yet some impulse bade me hasten toward the main door,
for I dared not neglect the possibility that I kept some hapless
caller in the downpour. I had not yet reached our sturdy door,
however, when I perceived the securely fastened latch,
noiselessly and by degrees, twisting as if by an unseen hand!
Thereupon, the latch clicked, and scarcely a moment after, the
sturdy door was thrust open, revealing the mysterious caller.

My God! the figure of horror that then trampled the
threshold—! I scarcely believe it even now, for I saw at once
that although my peculiar guest resembled a maiden aunt's
cherished Puss, this was no common tabby cat. I judged the
emaciated creature to stand at fully eight and three-quarters in
height; a tall, rotting hat of bygone fashion crowned its fell

head—and although unquestionably felid, the grotesque beast *stood upright, as if a man!*

My shock was incomplete, however, for without introduction, the vaguely human creature then addressed me familiarly, proposing that he should demonstrate certain forbidden rites—the very rites said to be once practiced by the ancient votaries of the impious Pnakotic Manuscripts!

At this, I started—alas! For the cunning brute had named none other than the prime subject of those same miscarried occult studies that my aged mother begged me to abandon. No doubt you will inquire whether filial duty compelled me to eject the unnatural creature at once; but the clever felid, discerning my hesitation, assured me that the gambit was wholesome, whereupon I yielded, agreeing to tolerate some part of his demonstration before rendering judgment.

However, my clever pet, Clara, who observed from the fastness of her cage, was less timid; she cried out furiously, almost as if urging me, if only for the sake of my trusting mam, to refuse our incredible guest. But at this, the uncouth felid's greenish eyes glittered with displeasure, and snatching up the cage containing my quavering pet, he bellowed that she should fear nothing. Thereupon, wildly gesticulating with his sinister hand as he shrieked in some barbarous tongue, he cried—

"Ub...ub...uppai...midi bridd...Nyarlathotep!"

I had not the time to protest before the brute released the cage!—but no disaster followed; instead, my poor, complaining Clara commenced a circumgyration of the fiend—*yet my pet remained securely within her cage!*

It does me no credit to confess that I protested this not at all—indeed, the demonstration thrilled me! Leering at the spectacle of my circumvoluting pet, my grotesque guest renewed his assurances that I had naught to fear. Then, with almost daemonic energy, and boasting of subsequent miracles, he leapt atop the ceramic gazing-globe that stood at hand, bidding me to watch. With further wild gesticulations, he again muttered the guttural formulae—after which, first the monograph I had laid aside, then my abandoned teacup, and finally, my half-eaten tea-cake, flew toward the gaunt felid and assumed orbit about his being!

An indescribable expression of wicked pride crept across my guest's features as he again bade me to witness his tricks; gesturing next toward the model of the *Emma* and the dish of creamer meant for my tea, the brute then gathered these into the bizarre orbit! But he was not done, for now innumerable of my virtuous mother's cherished mementos churned about him by means of the same blasphemous operation as before.

At last, his agitation compounding as he demanded I witness all he would show me, he compelled my delicate, Oriental fan to fly toward him, but this last, he snatched from the air, and seizing it with his mangy tail, he proceeded to leap and gibber, as if performing a profane ritual, all the while fanning himself with it!

What virtue can I claim when I tell you that the spectacle of my mother's most cherished mementoes churning about the abominable felid, who cackled as he hopped on one elongated foot atop the delicate globe, failed to elicit either my scepticism or outright condemnation? For alas, while my trepidation increased, the thrilling sight mesmerized me! I perceived that I alone of living men was witness to blasphemous secrets believed lost to time—the very same blasphemies that drove pious churchmen of a thousand years past to consign the Pnakotic Manuscripts to roaring bonfires—and these were but a small portion of what might yet be revealed, if I but held my tongue!

Meanwhile, the brute, now perceiving my anticipation, interrupted his rite to bleat in celebration and swear that I had yet to see all—but the words had hardly left his lips when the thrashing creature stumbled and capsized. No more than an instant later, his unnatural orbit of thieved prizes was arrested, and as I looked on in horror, they, too, collided with the floor!

Had this catastrophe injured my cherished Clara, I might have turned the fiend out at that moment. But God's hand was upon her, for it happened that in its descent, the door of her cage was struck by another of his prizes, thus freeing the latch, and once more renewing her objections to my loathsome guest's antics, the clever bird flew forth to hide herself in the teapot!

The fiend, meanwhile, squatted glumly on the rug as if disappointed by Clara's rebuke; indeed, I could almost believe my gentle turtledove was enumerating the creature's offences! I confess that I, too, shrank in disconsolation, for my promises to my absent mother rose again in my mind.

The monstrous felid, however, soon recovered himself, and springing upright, reiterated that he gained no small pleasure from his visit; moreover, he went on, he would not depart until he had revealed the sum of his wondrous knowledge, the next part of which demonstration would now commence.

Thus saying, he loped to our manor's sturdy door and flung it wide. Alas, although I was of a mind to bar his reentry, I was not quick enough, for in another moment, the cunning creature reappeared. On his slumping shoulders, however, he carried a prodigious, worm-eaten box of a vermillion hue such as only the morbid genius of Pickman might propose; this he shrugged to the floor, and surmounting it, his nictitating eyes glittered beneath his battered hat as he once again bade me observe.

Sealed for aeons within this box, he confided, were two indescribable specimens—beings unclassified by living men since the antediluvian flourishing of deserted Pnakotus! He was, however, sure that they would win my confidence, and assuring me that I should have no fear, he would release them from their prison that I might witness them.

Then, with a flick of his weirdly human hand, he unlatched the rotting box, and in an instant, entities unstudied by men of science flew frenetically forth! So unlike our familiar creeping and flying beasts were the deformed monsters that I can call them only *Things*—and yet, as they rushed forward, I swear they addressed me in our own noble tongue! So greatly baffled was I that I made no argument as the *Things* gestured, as if inviting me to friendship; but my ever-alert pet, Clara, who still sheltered in the antique tea-pot, cried out uselessly at this, as if begging me to turn them out.

Immediately, my hideous guest turned to my innocent Clara, an expression almost of indulgence on his face as he reiterated that we should fear nothing from his harmless pets, and so saying, he affectionately fondled the sickly creatures. Then, without further preamble, and still over my poor turtledove's shrill objections, he bade them freely frolic among my aged mother's cherished possessions!

It is impossible to precisely describe the impious servants which the *Things* then loosed into our once-orderly home; I may come closest by likening their forms to the familiar kites flown in the spring skies—yet if so, they were blasphemies of such innocent playthings! Propelled into the air by gossamer thread, the vaguely pteropodid accomplices were harlequin in pattern, with angular, membranous bodies stretched over vestigial skeletons. Moreover, their irregular shape, although evoking the familiar rhombus of my dreamy school days, contradicted all settled geometry—indeed, I can describe their form only as non-Euclidean!

Alas, in my stupefaction I delayed checking the *Things*' wretched battering, and already they loped toward my own mother's chambers. There, to my horror, they set upon profaning my poor dam's most intimate possessions, all the while shrieking with obscene glee! In another instant, their membranous companions had caught upon my virtuous mother's Sunday best, which now fluttered helplessly as the howling *Things* made a game of frenetically beating the very air with it! Yet the wicked game was not finished, for as the mindless rhomboids thrashed about my dam's chambers, they dared assail even my mother's neatly made bed in a cacophony of desecration!

This last was too much; my revulsion overcame me at last, and I trembled to think of the sorrow my disobedience would cause my virtuous mother—I shuddered, too, to consider the perils awaiting all mankind if I failed to banish my unwelcome guest and his fiendish *Things*, for what order of virtue would remain inviolate in the wake of this anarchic trinity?

I became aware then that poor Clara's cries had begun anew; at the next moment, the hall clock commenced striking. In my stupefaction, I had not noticed the time, but turning to the antique, I saw that my sweet turtledove had warned me well, for the hour of my mother's return was at hand! Indeed, in my agitation, I fancied the bird's cries announced the beat of the good woman's soles upon our walk, and comprehending that I must not delay, I therefore seized my butterfly net.

Assuring myself that so armed, I would overcome the *Things*, I lunged toward the slavering fiends—and to my glad surprise, my aim was true, for I discovered I had sealed the squealing imps securely in the sturdy frame! But I had not the luxury of rejoicing, for their hateful commander still hovered nearby, and thus turning on the horrible felid, I cried that he *would* obey me—that in God's name, he would shut his imps in their ancient sepulcher—that the three *would* abandon this place!

Dumbfounded, the creature squatted before me, despairing aloud that his demonstration had won neither my liking nor my allegiance; but the fierceness of my expression must have dissuaded him from persevering, for, chittering to himself, he drove the captured fiends back to their mouldering keep. Then, gathering the mildewed box to him, he cast me a final, sorrowful glance before slinking into the still-raging storm!

Grateful though I was that the horrible felid had vanished, Clara's renewed chatter called my attention to the destruction around me. It could not be undone before my worthy mother's return—it was impossible! I had, alas, no earthly means to remedy the consequences of my moral foeter! What choice had I but to confess the afternoon's events to my trusting mother?

But lo! At that moment, the figure of my departed guest reappeared in the entrance. I readied myself to utter a fresh invective, but he addressed me as before, explaining that it was not well to privilege the uninitiated with such secrets as he had revealed to me. He would, he continued, benefit me with one final miracle—a trick that would restore all to its former order.

So saying, he once again commenced muttering his indecipherable formulae, gesturing maniacally about him. By what means the unnatural felid performed his trick, I cannot say, but as I watched in mute astonishment, it seemed almost as if the indescribable operation were performed with mechanical precision and inhuman speed. For in less than a minute, the cake and tea service, my books, the model of my ancestor's ship, my mother's Sunday gown, and even poor, quavering Clara, all were plucked as if by a throng of unseen hands and renewed to their former stations!

At last, the creature's ministry completed, he turned to me a final time, whereupon, with an unsettling tip of his absurd top hat, he bade me an ominous farewell before fading into the deepening gloom.

Shaken and exhausted by the ordeal, I had time only to fall back into my familiar armchair; for hardly a moment had elapsed before I raised my eyes to recognize the figure of my own, tender dam entering the room. Oh, with what unsuspecting trust the poor woman addressed me! —how had I fared, she inquired; had I entertained myself well?

Alas! I hesitated, debating whether to confess my error and beg forgiveness; but as the kindly dowager looked upon me with an encouraging smile, I could discover no firm course of action. And in that moment, I comprehended that the afternoon's encounter, though but brief in time, had now permanently altered the course of my life—for what choice had I now but either to deceive the worthy woman who had tended me since infancy, or crush her maternal heart by admitting my disobedience?

You will ask, certainly, which course I chose; but here I must end my account. I can leave you only with this: what courage would remain of any rational man shockingly preyed upon by the foulest denizens of Hell? For I must live out the remainder of my life with the visions of what I have witnessed as my only company—the dreams I once thought only madness produced—and yet—they are no phantasies—I vow it, *the blasphemous trinity was utterly real!*

Identity

SHAUN HORTON

When Julie woke, the smell was the first thing she knew. Her nose was assaulted with the smell of blood and decay. Awareness of touch returned next, telling her she was bound to a chair, in a cold room.

She held her eyes shut, hoping that as long as she didn't see it, she could be convinced her other senses were lying. The strength of the smell continued to grow, creating a knot in her stomach as she tried not to vomit.

The sound of heavy boots coming down creaking, wooden stairs caught her attention next, forcing her to finally open her eyes. There was no holding back the contents of her stomach after that.

She was in a basement, although it looked like someone had tried to convert it into a half-assed butcher's shop or meat locker. The wall to her left was lined with box freezers, and in the center of the room was a large wooden table, made of thick planks. Next to her were more chairs, some with fragments of rope still attached to them. Everything, from the freezers, to the table, to the floor, was covered with stains, ranging from a dim red, to black.

Bloodstains.

The heavy footsteps descended on her right, and the sight of the man that stepped down the stairs made her tremble. He was over six feet tall, and heavily built, that much was obvious even under the raincoat he was wearing.

"Please don't struggle too much. I don't want you to get hurt." The voice was thick and spoke in a slow, methodical manner, as if every word was carefully examined and measured before it was allowed to leave his lips.

Julie started to cry, if this monster of a man didn't want her injured, it could only mean things even worse than death. Her eyes squinted shut as she sobbed, doing her best to ignore the sounds of his boots on the floor as he approached her.

Something soft touched her cheek, and her eyes flew open, her body jerking back from the touch. The man was kneeling in front of her, a handkerchief in one outstretched hand. He'd wiped away some of her tears. This close, she couldn't avoid seeing his face.

It was covered with scars, and looked mismatched. Julie wondered if he'd had a stroke, as one side of his face was so out of place next to the other. Even his eyes didn't belong together, one was deep brown, while the other was blue.

She looked down at the handkerchief; it was held by long, feminine fingers attached to a thick, swollen palm. Seeing the twisted thing before her was enough to jolt her out of her despair.

"There. There we go. No need to cry now." He stood up, tucked the handkerchief back into his pocket and turned to the table.

"What...what are you going to do with me?"

"I am sorry for taking you so forcefully last night. You looked like one that could help me, though."

"H-help you? With what? Why do you have me tied up like this to help you?"

"You would run away if I didn't. I just want someone to help me find out who I am."

He pulled a chair over next to her, then dragged around an extension cord. The long fingers pulled an electrical plug out from under his raincoat and connected it to the extension.

Then he sat down in the chair and looked at her. He pulled the handkerchief out again and gently dabbed at her lips and chin, wiping away the last vestiges of her vomit.

"I would tell you my name, but I honestly don't have one. Why don't you tell me yours?"

"J-Julie."

"That's a nice name. I bet it suits you very well. Can you tell me about yourself? What makes you a Julie?"

She started trembling again. If she stayed silent would he hit her? Beat her? If she told him, would he sell her off? Carted out of the country in a box to be some random man's sex toy?

"I...I'm twenty-six, engaged. My fiancé and I...were trying to get...pregnant." Julie tried to come up with some kind of story, something that he might take pity on and let her go.

The man just nodded. "I see. You must love your fiancé very much to say yes to marriage and to have a baby with him. So, you're straight, then? Or maybe bi?"

"I...I'm...bi. I like women, but I love my fiancé too." Maybe she could get sold to a woman; she couldn't imagine that wouldn't be preferable to being owned by some strange, rich, man.

"I see. What about your hobbies? Your job? Do you like animals?"

The questions were starting to throw her off now. People who sold you into the sex trade didn't seem like the kind of people who cared about the things you enjoyed.

"I like animals. I used to volunteer at an animal rescue group. We took in stray dogs and cats, cleaned them up and then found them good homes."

He smiled a little bit, his face twisting unnaturally around the scars. "I like that. I don't know much about myself, but I know I like animals. At least, most of me likes animals."

"Are you...looking for people who share your interests? There's websites to meet and talk to people and groups at the library, or you could take classes at college or..."

He held up his other hand, a gesture that was obviously meant to stop her rambling. Like the rest of him, this hand didn't match either. Instead of long, slender fingers, this hand, his left, had fingers that were short and pudgy. The two middle fingers and thumb were shades of purple, like they were heavily bruised, or even broken. He suddenly seemed to notice that she was staring at his fingers and quickly withdrew his hand back under the raincoat.

"Sorry about that. My left hand is unpleasant to look at right now.

"I've told you about me, like you asked. Tell me something about you now. It's only fair."

Julie still had no idea what he wanted her for. This wasn't adding up to a kidnapping, and he certainly wasn't acting like he planned to kill her. There was no way she could ignore all the dried blood around the room though...

"Well, I suppose. I like you enough now. I think you'll fit in. I don't know who I am. I'm trying to find myself. It's hard when everyone is so different though. I see little pieces of myself in other people, but then in other ways we couldn't be more different. I don't understand how that works."

He slowly stood up and walked over to the table, the extension cord following him. The giant stood there a moment, then grabbed the raincoat and pulled it over his head and off. His back was a mass of scars, along with a rainbow of different skin tones and bruises. There was a fresh incision around his right side that still had sutures holding it closed, even as a thin line of pus flowed down his back from it. The plug that he had stuck into the extension cord was clearly visible now, the wires running up his back and disappearing under his skin.

The slender fingers of his right hand reached back and pointed to a patch of skin that seemed to stretch from just under his shoulder to down below the waistband of his sweatpants.

"This was John Harmon. He liked animals too. He was forty-two and worked as a bartender. He also had a daughter, and two grandsons."

Julie's eyes widened as she noticed the scars on his back made a circle around the skin the giant was pointing at. He turned, and she saw his entire body was a patchwork of different skins. The left side of his chest was muscular and covered with dark hair, while the right had a breast that sagged heavily. The swollen left hand pointed at the breast next.

"This was Sarena. She wouldn't tell me her last name, but she did like animals. She was lazy though. No schooling, no work, she only wanted to marry a rich man."

He walked over to the freezers now as he talked, the extension cord following him, staying plugged into the cord coming out of his back. He dug through the freezer on the end, eventually holding up a bag of blood.

"Do you happen to know your blood type, Julie? It's okay if you don't. Seems like most people don't."

He pulled out a different bag and set it on the table, before going over to a cabinet in the corner and rummaging through it.

"But yes, most of me likes animals a lot, so I think you'll fit in pretty well. That really seems to be the thing that brings most of me together."

"What the fuck are you?" Julie's voice trembled as she watched him walk around the room, collecting various tools and setting them on the table.

"What am I? That I can answer. I am a product of the people around me. When I was first born, I was only made up of four men. But some parts didn't fit, or didn't feel right, so I've been trying to find the right mix of people to create the real 'me'. Since I was born, I've tried adding in parts from 173 people. Men. Women. The oldest was sixty-four. The youngest was sixteen. Straight, bi, gay. If I'm going to be honest, that's probably the easiest. I'm probably bi, because why limit yourself to one side or the other?"

He laid out the tools on the table.

"Unfortunately, most of the parts don't last. You saw my left hand. That was Samuel Carter. He was twenty-eight, gay, liked dogs, but not cats, overweight. He was a hematologist, but had been out of work for three years."

The giant stood at the table again, his back to Julie. He lifted a large cleaver, and slammed it onto the table. When he turned around again, the part of his left hand which had been Samuel Carter was gone, cut clean off. A mix of blood, pus, and thick, brown sludge oozed from the wound. Then he was approaching her with the cleaver and a rubber strap. The slender fingers of his right hand grabbed her arm, and Julie felt how cold his touch was, like he wasn't a living thing.

He pulled out her left arm, tying the rubber strap tightly around the bicep. Then he grabbed her hand, spreading the fingers in the middle. In a move that was as smooth as could be, he lifted the cleaver and brought it down on her hand, severing the top half with her thumb and first two fingers.

Julie screamed as the pain flooded through her body, the strap slowing the bleeding, but still letting enough through to spurt in time with her heartbeat. He grabbed the strap and tightened it down even more before taking the severed hand and returning to the table.

Julie bit down on her lip, trying to do everything she could to not go into shock. Already she was getting light-headed, and the room was starting to spin. Then searing pain shot up her left arm again and she went limp.

The first thing she noticed when she woke up was the throbbing headache she had. Slowly, Julie opened her eyes, praying the last time she opened them had just been a doozy of a nightmare after a long, rough night of drinking. The throbbing in her left hand told her otherwise. Something was poking into her right arm. She turned to look and saw a catheter had been inserted, and was attached to a bag of blood that hung from the wall. Reluctantly, she turned to look at her left hand. All that was left was the pinky and ring finger, the rest was gone, and the huge wound it had left behind was charred and burned like someone had tried to cauterize it.

She screamed.

The giant came down the stairs.

"You're awake. That's good. I was hoping I got the blood stopped soon enough." He smiled, and held up his left hand. The swollen, purple fingers of Samuel Carter were gone, in their place were tan, slender fingers, held in place with a mixture of staples and sutures. Blood and pus oozed out along the seam, but somehow the fingers and thumb flexed and moved. "Looks like we get along well, after all."

Julie wanted to scream; but a knot had formed in her throat, making her gag. Her body convulsed, twisting in the chair. The giant came over, looking concerned. He reached out for her, and Julie tried to twist away from his disgusting, jigsaw-puzzle hand even as a new wave of convulsions started in her guts. The combination sent the chair over to one side with a crunch, the extra distance ripping the catheter out of her arm and adding a new spray of blood to the floor.

Then the giant's hands were on her, strong but gentle and firm; and cold as ice. He righted the chair, and set about stopping the blood that was oozing from her arm. She just sat there, gasping for breath.

"Please don't panic, I need your help. I need you to tell me who I am. Who we are."

Julie couldn't answer if she wanted to, she just sat there and let the giant move her arm, wrapping it up in gauze.

"Just rest for now. I want to talk to you more, and I'll bring down some food later if you think you can handle it."

Her head hung limp as she sat there, and with what little breath she had recovered, she sobbed. The giant stood there a minute, then slowly went back upstairs, leaving Julie alone.

She knew her life was over. The giant was going to take her apart, piece by piece, and replace his own slowly rotting parts. The best she could hope for was that she could die with the next piece he took. Maybe an arm, or a leg, something where she could quickly bleed out before he could stop it.

Her weight shifted to the right, settling into the chair. It creaked. She glanced over, not willing to believe the sound was anything but an old piece of furniture groaning at even her meager weight.

The chair's arm was split and cracked. It wasn't broken, but the fall had definitely damaged it. Julie wiggled, her arm throbbing where the catheter had torn out. The chair's arm wiggled with her. She stared at it, trying to figure out what she could do to break the arm enough to get free. Another hard fall might do it, but it would bring the giant back, and if it cracked further but didn't break, he might notice it. Even if it broke, she would need time to get free from the rest of the ropes.

Part of her wanted to just give in to despair, settle into the chair and accept her fate; but there was a small ball of heat in her chest, a smoldering rage that wanted to hurt the giant, that wouldn't let her.

Before she even realized it, Julie shifted her weight to the left, then threw herself back to the right as hard as she could, pulling the chair over and smashing onto the floor. The chair hit with a crunch.

Julie wiggled her arm, testing the chair. The arm had broken off and was in her hand. She could already hear steps on the floor above her, but excitement flooded through her now. One hand being free gave her enough space to wiggle around the rope which tied her to the back of the chair. She could easily get free if she just had enough time.

The heavy steps were coming down the stairs.

She let herself go limp, hoping he wouldn't notice the broken arm right away or how loose the rope around her chest was. She heard him sigh as he saw her.

She felt him lift her up and set the chair back on its feet. "Oh, look what you did..." He was leaning down and inspecting the broken arm of the chair. Julie was almost too scared to move, but as he leaned in, she took the broken arm in her hand and jammed it into his face.

The giant fell back, clutching at his face, and Julie was suddenly in a frenzy, worming her way out of the rope which held her to the chair and clawing at the large knots that held her other hand and feet. Free, she moved towards the stairs, but felt the giant grab one of her ankles.

"I wish you hadn't done that, now I have to replace that eye."

The grip on her ankle was the slender feminine fingers of his right hand, but the grip was impossibly strong. She looked down and the piece of the chair was jutting out of his face, pus and blood leaking out around it and running down his face. She spun around and stomped on his forearm, over and over trying to get him to release his hold.

"Let. Me. GO!"

She kicked out at his face next. He was a mountain of a man, but he was on the ground while she was on her feet; she connected with the piece of wood sticking out of his right eye, jarring it and pushing it deeper, finally getting a grunt out of him.

"I can't let you go, Julie. You are a part of me now, I need you to stay."

He looked up at her with his one eye, his face expressionless under the scars and the fluids that covered half of it. Julie was a mix of disgust, rage, and fear at the complete lack of anger and the matter-of-factness in his voice, even with the piece of wood still sticking out of his face.

Julie grabbed the cleaver off the table, swinging it as hard as she could in one hand, hacking at the hand that still clutched her ankle. Nothing spurted, he didn't howl in pain, just more of the disgusting mixture flowing from the wounds, pooling on the floor as Julie swung over and over. She started screaming as all her emotions broke free. Then she could finally pull her leg away, the severed hand still clutching her.

"Julie, please, you are a part of me. Help me understand us…"

"Understand this, you Frankenstein freak!" Julie continued screaming as she stepped back in reach of the giant as he reached for her with his other hand, swinging the cleaver and hacking at his face. He just looked up at her with his one eye, expressionless as she sliced up his face and head. He was pushing himself up with the oozing stump of his right hand as he reached for her with his left, almost unfazed by her hacking at him. Julie grabbed his left hand by the wrist and slammed it against the top of the table.

"And give me back my fucking hand!"

The cleaver plowed through the giant's wrist, separating his left hand cleanly. She grabbed the hand and ran back and up the stairs, leaving him on the floor.

Upstairs was an old house, badly neglected and empty, but she quickly found the front door and dashed outside, the sun blinding her.

For the first time, she noticed how clear and clean the air smelled, and when she could see, she recognized where she was. It was an old housing project which the development had fallen through. A few other houses stood around in partial states of completion, but the road led out to a main street.

Julie paused to pry off the hand which still hung onto her ankle, and hobbled down the road, still clutching the hand that

had her old fingers and thumb. She wondered if they could still
be reattached.

Tulpa Pebbles

DANIEL S. DUVALL

Gary Dillon, age six, walked alone down the sidewalk on the block where he and Mommy, Daddy, and Tim lived. Tim was the best brother. He delighted in teaching Gary all about the trees and shrubs one could find along their street; they lived in Bagan Township within Ohio's Lorain County, where Wild Plum and Yellow Birch trees were plentiful and Bladdernut Shrubs decorated many suburban yards.

En route to his best friend Andy's house, Gary paused to admire an American Chestnut. Tim had taught him that in the distant past, Native Americans had used the nuts from this tree as both a food and a medicine. Tim knew all about history. Gary admired his brother's sharp mind.

Gary found Colleen, Andy's teen sister, waiting for him further up the sidewalk. She often babysat her little brother and his friends.

"You're always totally punctual," Colleen said. She often used words that Gary didn't know, but she always took the time to explain if he asked. He opted to learn about "punctual" later, as he was eager to see Andy's new Hot Wheels.

Colleen, whose waist-length hair always smelled of coconut shampoo, took Gary's hand and led him across the freshly-mowed lawn toward her two-story abode.

She said, "Your brother should have walked you down here."

"He wants to help me be indepanda."

"Independent?"

"That's it."

"Fine, but you're still a little tyke, and the world's full of unpredictable dangers."

Gary shrugged off her words and bounded up the porch steps with thoughts of die-cast vehicles flooding his imagination.

Indoors, as Gary scampered up the staircase toward Andy's bedroom, he overheard Colleen using her cell phone to talk with someone (perhaps that mean boy named Brian who, Gary knew, was not supposed to be around without adult supervision). Colleen seemed to be inviting him over. Gary instinctively feared Brian.

Andy, in his typically manic way, pushed a yellow Ford Mustang around the floor and said, "It's not fair that you get two birthdays every year."

Gary, who had celebrated his sixth birthday exactly six months earlier and thus was looking forward to his "six and a half" party later that afternoon, gawked at the goldfish that swam in a bowl atop Andy's nightstand. "It's tradition," he said. Tim had taught him the meaning of that last word toward the end of winter.

Andy stood, pointed at the fish, and proclaimed, "I have dreams about him talking with me."

"What does he say?"

"Weird stuff. Like, I need more Scooby Doo posters. And that I should get another fish to keep him company."

Colleen poked her head in the doorway and said, "Almost time for Gary to go home."

As Andy made a beeline back to the house to fetch some frozen treats, Gary stood next to Colleen near the sidewalk and frowned at the puffy August clouds overhead. He pointed.

"I can see the silver right there," he said. Colleen laughed. She was a decade older than Gary. She crouched and looked the tot in the eye.

Colleen said, "Clouds don't actually contain silver. That saying about a lining isn't literally true. Do you know that word? Literal?"

Gary acknowledged that he was unfamiliar with the term.

Brian, Colleen's boyfriend, sneered. Gary noted how much his puckered mouth and soulless eyes resembled the face of the goldfish.

Brian said, "He's too young to understand that. Also, he's not the smartest little guy, is he? Dumbness runs in his family."

Gary wanted to cry, and Colleen saw the look on his face. She stood and swatted Brian's shoulder. "You're verbally abusive," she said.

"Yet you continue to make out with me."

Andy, who had just returned with two ice lollies, rolled his eyes. "I know what making out is," he said.

"Do tell," prodded Brian.

"It's where babies come from."

Brian made eye contact with Colleen and said, "I see these two are intellectual equals."

Gary tuned out the conversation as Colleen admonished Brian for his nasty comments. He thought about what Uncle Lloyd had told him: "Every cloud has a silver lining." He'd said so at Aunt Marnie's funeral. Ever since, Gary had scanned the skies and pondered why silver, which even he knew was heavier than air, didn't just fall right down to the ground.

He didn't know what Colleen meant with that word "literal," but he knew that Brian was a "bully." Tim had taught him about bullies and told him that if he encountered any, he should tell a trusted adult.

Andy handed one of the frozen treats to Gary and asked,

"Want to see my goldfish again?"

Gary checked his digital watch (a gift from Uncle Lloyd) and said, "I'll visit the fish next time. Thanks for the ice lolly."

He looked to Colleen and tapped his watch (a behavior he'd picked up by imitating his father).

Brian kissed his gal farewell and hopped on his rusty bike. He lived two blocks over and could walk, but Gary figured the bully enjoyed showing off his fancy ride.

Colleen looked at Andy and said, "You're coming with us."

"I could stay inside by myself."

"Mother and Father would disown me if I left you home alone. Let's go." Andy sighed and took his sister's hand.

Brian asked Colleen, "See you tonight?"

"Unless you get grounded."

Brian smiled, and Gary noted that even the bully's grin had a sneer-like quality.

"Colleen is correct: there is not really silver in clouds." Tim told Gary as the siblings sat side-by-side on their front porch. Tim had been teaching Gary about different types of birds that summer, and they had already spotted two robins and a blue jay. Inside, their folks (assisted by Uncle Lloyd) were setting up for the party.

"But Uncle Lloyd told me so," protested Gary.

"There are things called 'figures of speech.' What 'every cloud has a silver lining' really means is that every bad thing in life has some good aspect too."

"Clouds are bad? What's an 'aspect?'"

"Clouds aren't inherently bad," said Tim, who at the age of eleven prided himself on his vocabulary. "But whoever made up that saying must have not liked rain. I guess what I'm trying to explain is that when something makes you cry, you should examine it and find something about it that makes you smile."

Gary sat silently and gazed up and down the street as he

pondered his brother's words. He thought he got most of it, but up until just then he'd thought there was silver in clouds.

Gary was grateful to his brother for at least trying to explain how the world worked. Tim was a gentle and loving brother.

Gary hoped that Brian had no siblings.

An avian visitor hopped through the grass.

"There's a...starling?"

"Very good," said Tim.

The front door opened, and there stood Mommy. "Time to celebrate," she said. Gary clapped his hands, smiled, and ran inside.

Gary thoroughly enjoyed his party, which included the unwrapping of four nifty presents (one each from Daddy, Mommy, Tim, and Uncle Lloyd) and the consumption of hot chocolate (despite the summer heat, Gary insisted on having his favorite beverage).

The family played a game of tag out in the front yard, and Gary giggled and had a grand time even though he knew that Tim was letting him catch and tag him.

Then it was time for dinner, and Daddy served mac and cheese sprinkled with a bit of Old Bay seasoning (just the way Gary liked it).

After the meal, Uncle Lloyd read to Gary. They got all the way through the first chapter of a book called *The Great Brain* that Tim had enjoyed back in July. Gary, rapt, listened to his uncle's deep voice intone the adventures of the Fitzgerald brothers. Gary knew he'd want to read the rest of the book himself when he got older. He'd ask Tim to read chapter two that night.

After story time, Mommy's cell phone rang. She'd been summoned to work (she served coffee at The Sentient Mammal down on Front Street in Wallace Falls over in Cuyahoga

County); another barista had called in sick.

Daddy asked Uncle Lloyd if he'd watch Gary and Tim while he drove his wife to her job (Mommy had a clinical aversion to driving herself). Lloyd said sure, and so Gary and Tim found themselves alone with their uncle (who at the age of fifty was the oldest person Gary knew aside from his grandparents).

"I have a very special gift for both of you," Uncle Lloyd said, and Gary's eyes lit up.

"More presents?"

"One for you and one for Tim. I brought these along in case I got a chance to talk to the two of you out of earshot of your folks."

Tim climbed out of his bean bag chair in the corner and ambled over to the sofa where Lloyd and Gary sat. His uncle's words had him intrigued.

Lloyd reached into a pocket and pulled out two bluish-green pebbles. No more than an inch long, both stones looked as if they'd been hand-polished. Lloyd held the pebbles in his open palm and withdrew his hand when Gary reached for one.

"I have to explain exactly what these are," Lloyd said. "You can look, but don't touch yet."

Gary studied the gifts. They were pretty, like Mommy's eyes, but he didn't know what he'd do with his except set it on his nightstand and look at it.

"These are called Tulpa Pebbles," said Lloyd. "I don't reckon either of you have ever heard of a tulpa before." He looked at his nephews, who stared back with blank faces. "I got these in Tibet, where the notion of tulpas originated."

Tim asked, "When did you go to Tibet?" Neither Mommy nor Daddy had said anything about Lloyd traveling.

"Before you were born," said Lloyd. "I've held onto these a long time, and I've never had reason nor courage to try to use them. I have three more at home, and I plan to finally test them out myself. Come what may, I'll try." Lloyd laughed nervously.

Gary asked, "Use them how?"

"Tulpa Pebbles supposedly have magical properties."

"Properties?"

Tim said, "Aspects."

"Powers," said Lloyd. "They've been enchanted in such a way that they help focus one's imagination to the point where one can summon forth something you visualize into the real world."

Gary and Tim took a moment to think.

Tim asked, "Summon what, exactly?"

"Anything you can dream up. Could be in the form of a person, or an object, or even a whole building. I don't...I'm not sure I believe in tulpas, but I have an old friend in Tibet who swears..."

Gary didn't pay attention to the rest of what his uncle said, for his mind was racing with ideas about how he'd use his pebble. He'd always wanted a pet. Maybe he'd create just the sort of Collie he'd like to befriend. Or he could make his very own house out on the lawn. Or a spaceship.

"One last thing," Lloyd said. "These will work once apiece, and then they're done. You can't summon more than one tulpa. So make sure you're certain of what you want before you use 'em."

Tim asked, "How do they work?"

Lloyd said, "You first clear your mind. Like, sit in a dim room and try to think about nothing for an hour. Have the pebble sitting where you want your tulpa to materialize; it need not be near you, but it can be. Then you start to visualize your tulpa in vivid detail. Make it as real in your mind as you can."

Gary and Tim hung on Lloyd's every word.

"Then you pretend you're pushing it out of your head. Keep your eyes closed throughout all of this, by the way. Supposedly when the tulpa springs out into reality, you'll know it. You'll feel it exit your mind and manifest externally." Lloyd chuckled. "This is probably all a tall tale that some snake oil salesman told me."

Tim asked, "Why haven't you ever tried one?"

Lloyd said, "If I did and it worked, I'd be forced to accept the existence of magic, and I've always felt I'd lose my mind if that happened."

Gary thought he'd settled on his ideal tulpa (an ice cream dispenser that could generate infinite amounts of any flavor) when his uncle handed him one pebble.

"Use this carefully," Lloyd said. "In case it's real."

Gary squeezed it between two fingers and held it close to his face as Lloyd gave the other Tulpa Pebble to Tim.

"Why let us have these?" Tim asked.

"I wish I'd had a chance to discover real magic when I was your age. I would've been able to handle it and not go insane. Young minds are exceptionally flexible."

Gary didn't follow that at all, but he didn't care. He had a Tulpa Pebble, and he was certain it would work. It had to. He knew magic was real. It's how Santa Claus could travel around the whole world in just a few hours.

Gary and Tim hid their pebbles under their respective mattresses. Lloyd had advised them to keep the plan to summon tulpas to themselves "lest your parents ship me off to an institution." Gary and Tim had laughed, and after dark they said farewell to Uncle Lloyd (who took a taxi back to his Cleveland apartment). Daddy was home by then, but Mommy would be slinging espresso until midnight and would catch a ride home with a manager.

Tim had made Gary promise not to use his pebble until at least the next day. "We have to think really carefully before we make our tulpas," Tim had said in his serious voice, and Gary nodded in agreement. Inwardly, he was sure he could use that ice cream machine that night, but he kept his promise to his brother.

The next day, Gary sat on the front porch with Tim, who read him chapter three of *The Great Brain*.

The bully came down the street on his bicycle, and Gary made the mistake of establishing eye contact. Brian stopped and studied the siblings, then yelled, "Physical books are so not cool. Save some trees and go electronic."

Tim sized up the teen and decided to ignore him. He and Gary got another two sentences into the story when Brian bellowed, "I'm talking to you, Medium Dillon."

Tim set down the book and stood up. Gary asked, "Should I get Dad?" Tim shook his head no.

Brian, who had initiated four arguments with Tim across the previous two months just for the sake of antagonizing the younger kid, wheeled his bike up the driveway. Tim walked toward him and said, "You're not welcome here."

Brian leaned his bicycle on its kickstand. "But I enjoy studying you and your brother," he said. "You're like monkeys in the zoo. I find your primitive behaviors fascinating."

"Tim," said Gary with fear in his voice. He could see that Brian was particularly amped up this afternoon. Andy had told Gary that Brian had flattened an older kid on the playground. Gary didn't want to see his brother provoke the bully.

"Primates have been known to fling their own feces at other animals," said Tim. He maintained eye contact with Brian. "You already smell like shit, so I won't bother."

Brian snorted and sneered and said, "Maybe I'll tell your parents about the language you use."

Tim asked, "Who do you reckon they'll believe? Me or the neighborhood delinquent who got caught stealing a bra off of Ms. Nakano's clothesline?"

Tim didn't even see the sucker-punch coming.

Gary gasped and watched, horrified, as Timmy lost his balance and collapsed to the driveway. He ran into the house and yelled for Mommy and Daddy.

Brian was long gone by the time Gary rushed to his brother's side with his parents in tow. Tim was sitting in the driveway with his palm held over his right eye, and he was rocking and crying.

Mommy dialed her cell phone while Daddy assessed the extent of his son's injuries: a swollen black eye, a scrape on his left leg, and a bruised ego.

Gary gazed at his wounded brother and decided right then and there how he'd use his Tulpa Pebble. The magical ice cream dispenser was no longer a priority.

At dusk, Gary and Tim sat on the porch with a box of baking soda and a bottle of vinegar. Tim had introduced his brother to the wonders of mixing these substances the week before, and Gary loved to feel the squishy goop-residue after each experiment.

Gary had sculpted a sphere last time, but he had a different form in mind now: a scale model of the scariest monster he could envision.

His tulpa would fix Brian but good.

Tim dumped a third of the baking soda into a plastic mixing bowl, then handed the vinegar to Gary and said, "Do the honors."

Gary grinned and poured some liquid. A foaming white substance bubbled up and over the bowl's edge and cascaded to the gray cement surface of the porch. Tim inhaled deeply and said, "I love that smell."

Gary waited for the mixture to settle down, and then he reached into the bowl and pulled out a handful of wet baking soda. He scooted down and set about molding something on the second porch step. He reached back for more goop and added it to his creation. Tim asked, "You sure you want to try this?"

Gary nodded. From his pocket, he pulled out his Tulpa Pebble. He stuck it in the middle of his sculpture, which resembled a sloppy gingerbread man. He and Tim smiled at each other and headed inside.

Gary retired to his bedroom an hour earlier than usual that night. He told his parents he was worn out and ready to sleep, but after they'd tucked him in, he cleared his mind for sixty minutes and then focused on the tulpa. He felt excited, and his belly had that tingle that he'd experienced the previous Christmas Eve. He pictured the tulpa's arms and legs and head and chest, and then he set about visualizing its fangs.

Tim had a view of the front porch from his bedroom window, and he stared at the little man his brother had sculpted and waited for something to happen. His gut told him that the Tulpa Pebbles were probably not magical, but he retained enough childlike optimism to hope that he might have an extraordinary night.

He was gearing up to crawl into bed when the baking soda man began to grow. Tim blinked and rubbed his eyes and looked again and wondered what manner of optical illusion could produce this effect. Then he allowed himself to believe, and he smiled and looked on in wonder as the monster outside took shape.

After a mere three minutes of rapid growth, the bipedal thing stood directly outside the house. It looked like an abominable snowman that had been injected with horse steroids: muscular and hulking and all of twelve feet tall. It flexed its claws and gazed at the street with a vulpine face complete with a fang-lined snout. It shambled down the middle of the empty street, and Tim watched until it vanished around the corner.

Brian smelled it before he saw it. He wondered who the hell had spilled vinegar in his room while he was sleeping, and then he heard his window shatter. He looked up just in time to see the creature's claw as it wrapped around his waist. Then he was yelling for help, and then the giant thing pulled him out through the frame that was edged with jagged glass, and Brian kept on screaming until its fangs tore out his throat.

Uncle Lloyd opened his eyes and gazed at the pile of Tulpa Pebbles in his living room. He'd sat on the couch and visualized a mountain of hundreds of the blue stones, and here they were. *If a genie grants you a wish,* he thought, *wish for more wishes.* He grabbed a handful of pebbles and cackled madly.

His mind had snapped when he saw the thing on the television news as it shambled down the street with the remnants of a teen's body slung over one of its shoulders. He'd realized at once that one of his nephews had summoned this particular tulpa. He'd known then that the magic was real.

Two hours later, Lloyd created a tulpa in the form of Marnie, his late wife.

Tim and Gary kept their mouths shut about the origin of the monster. Forty-five minutes after he'd created the monster, Gary had caused it to dissipate into a massive mound of wet baking soda simply by visualizing it doing so.

Authorities and scientists were baffled and spooked by the occurrence, and Brian's parents attended church every day for the rest of their lives on the assumption that their sins had brought forth a demon to take away their child.

Many who investigated Brian's death simply went nuts as

their minds tried to process what the evidence suggested: that a being made of vinegar-soaked baking soda had manifested and murdered a teen and then sat under an oak tree seemingly catatonic before it dissipated. There was plenty of documentation: cell phone recordings, professional news footage, and photographs. Assorted conspiracy theories sprang up: some swore that the thing had been a military construct made with nanotechnology, while others felt the being's existence had to be supernatural in origin.

The incident put Bagan Township on the global map.

Tim never did use his Tulpa Pebble, but Uncle Lloyd routinely made Marnies. Each tulpa existed for up to three days and then dissolved away like a psychedelic hallucination. Lloyd considered using the pebbles to create other things but decided he was grateful simply to enjoy the company of something that at least resembled his late wife. He kept the tulpas hidden in his upstairs bedroom with the curtains constantly drawn. The neighbors never suspected a thing.

Gary grew up to be a narcissistic sociopath. He'd enjoyed his first taste of revenge and had felt not one twinge of guilt about Brian's bloody death. He never again used a Tulpa Pebble, but he did study Tibetan mythology extensively from his undergrad days on through his first MFA degree. He kept an exhaustive collection of news reports about the monster that had appeared in his neighborhood and processed them over and over. His doctoral thesis, an analysis of how "The Bagan Township Entity" was perceived around the globe, served as the basis for a non-fiction book that enjoyed modest commercial success.

One afternoon as Gary sipped tea and brainstormed ideas for his second book, he wondered if he would have grown up with a conscience if Uncle Lloyd hadn't given him the Tulpa Pebble.

He was fairly certain that he would have. He rather enjoyed being a sociopath, though, even if it had cost him his relationships with his brother and parents. *Every cloud has a silver lining,* he thought, and giggled.

Dawn of the Bodysnatchers

ROGER JACKSON

The man hadn't told them his name, but Karl knew who he was well enough, even before he saw the leather bag.

He'd looked out of place as soon as he entered the tavern, that much was certain. The rich material and elegant stitching of his clothes marked him out as a gentleman, and his bearing, his straight-backed confidence, had made him look taller than he was, and taller still when the other patrons hunched themselves over their ales or their card games to avoid his gaze. Only one of the serving girls approached him, and he'd waved her away with a gloved hand, his cold blue eyes narrowing as he peered through the tavern's drifting shrouds of pipe smoke until he found the table where Karl and his brother Hans were waiting.

He'd strode over to them and sat, setting his bag down on the floorboards. He'd offered to buy them both another drink, and Hans had leaned forward, ready to accept, but Karl had quietened his brother with a shake of the head. He knew why this mysterious doctor had been looking for them, and didn't care to have his senses dulled by ale when he was discussing business.

As the doctor spoke, making his offer in hushed tones, he peeled off his gloves, and Karl took note of how smooth and clean his hands were, a gentleman's hands. Pale and fine-boned, very different from his own, with their scars and blunt fingers, the ragged nails silted with soil. There was a scent to the doctor's hands too, something that filtered through the pipe smoke to make Karl's nose itch. The scent of fine, expensive soaps, and beneath that, the sharp kiss of garlic.

Karl recognised the spice at once. Like all the townspeople, he'd grown up with the stink of it in his nostrils, hung upon doors and around necks, protection should the creatures that roamed the woods and mountains ever venture into the town to feed. So prevalent was the scent in Karl's life that he might not have noticed it at all but for its incongruity upon this refined man of medicine.

Karl had nodded at the man's words, his mouth curving into a little smile when the doctor drew a small sack of coins from the pocket of his overcoat and placed it upon the table. He noticed how the doctor's shoulders tightened a little as he brought out the gold, how one of his hands was starting to bunch into a bony fist, the fingertips of his other hand resting on the rough weft of the sack. Karl imagined that the man was suddenly very aware of how he'd unveiled the wealth in what he no doubt believed was a den of cutthroats and thieves, and if the truth be told Herr Doctor was absolutely correct. Karl saw how some of the tavern's other patrons turned their heads to look as they heard even the tiny jingle of gold against gold as the coins settled in the sack, but a glance from him and they turned away. He was well known in the town as a man not to be crossed, and this business, this hollow-cheeked sawbones with his fine clothes and his gold, were his now.

The doctor looked cautious but unafraid, and grudgingly Karl found himself respecting that. He'd heard tell of the doctor's exploits for many years, tales that had made him as much of a legend as the devils he hunted, and now Karl stared into the other man's ice-hued eyes beneath their noble brow, wondering if he might see the spark that made this narrow-shouldered figure such a force to be reckoned with. He saw nothing but a cold curiosity, and realised that he wasn't the only one gauging what kind of fellow he was doing business with.

'You'll do it?' the doctor asked. His fingertips pressed down lightly upon the gold.

Hans leaned forward again, beginning to nod, but Karl said, 'No.'

The doctor's eyebrows twitched upwards. 'No?'

'No,' Karl said again. He jerked his unshaven chin at the sack on the table. 'Not for so little a tally.'

The doctor shook his head. 'I think you'll find this is a sufficient—'

'My brother has a family,' Karl said. He smiled ruefully at Hans as he continued. 'He works hard, but gets paid little in return. Most nights, his children go to bed with empty bellies while you...' The smile faded as Karl returned his gaze to the doctor. 'You feast at your table of meat and wine. So, I reject your offer as *not* sufficient.'

The doctor's blue eyes narrowed as he turned to Hans. 'And what of you? As your brother says you work hard for so little. Will you let him throw away the chance to have gold in your pocket, to give your family at least something? What have you to say?'

Karl spoke to Hans, but his eyes never left the doctor's face. 'Show him.'

Hans leaned forward again, his lips parting so that he might extend the frayed stump of his tongue to the doctor. It slid from between his blackened teeth like a piece of chewed steak.

Karl had expected the doctor to gasp, to recoil in horror, but the man simply regarded the stump with the calm curiosity of a man of medicine. 'What happened?'

'Our father disapproved of his singing,' Karl told him as

Hans closed his mouth once more. 'And so one day he put his hunting knife to what he called good use. I disapproved of my father, and so the same day I made good use of mine.'

'I'm sorry,' the doctor said. 'But it would seem our business here is concluded.' His long fingers folded around the sack of gold. 'I'm sure I shall find new associates in the town.'

'No, you will not, Herr Doctor,' Karl told him. 'We have been seen together. No one else will help you. They will be too curious, too afraid to work for you when I would not. However...' He smiled. 'If you we're to double what you offer me now, then we may be able to come to some agreement.'

The doctor paused, considering. Finally, he nodded.

'Very well.' he said. 'This sack now, the other half when our task is completed.'

'And how do I know I can trust you?'

The doctor's thin lips twitched upwards in a smile as he pushed the sack of gold across the table. 'Of course you can trust me. I'm a doctor.'

Karl laughed, plucking the sack from where it sat and tucking it into his tunic. 'When do we start?'

'Tomorrow, at dawn,' the doctor told him. 'Make the necessary preparations and meet me at the gates to the graveyard.'

'Dawn? Karl shook his head. 'That's no time for grave-robbing.'

The doctor only smiled again. 'Strictly speaking, we're breaking into a crypt, not a grave, and believe me, the hour is well chosen.'

Karl opened his mouth to argue further, but the weight of the gold against his heart and the knowledge that there was more to come turned his words into a slow nod. He thought himself a sharp-witted sort, a survivor, but he knew in this case he'd do well to heed the wisdom of this strange doctor.

'Good.' The doctor leaned down to pluck his leather bag

from the floor. He set it on the table before him as he stood and put on his gloves.

He nodded in farewell and left the tavern, sweeping his doctor's bag from the table, but not before Karl had noted the inscription printed upon the leather in fading gold script, a confirmation he didn't need.

Dr. A. Van Helsing.

The sun was rising, though you wouldn't know it, Karl thought. He'd awoken to find the town wreathed in rolling veils of white mist, filling the air as it if it were bleeding from the brickwork of every house, seeping from between the cobbles of every lane. He thought it would have burned off by the time Hans harnessed the horse to their cart, but no; even as they drew near to the gates of the graveyard and saw Van Helsing waiting for them, his leather bag in one hand and his pocket watch in the other, the mist seemed to have thickened. It settled on Karl's shoulders, mingled with the sweat at his temples. He glanced to where Hans sat beside him, holding the reins, and found his brother's broad bulk little more than a grey silhouette. He might not have been there at all but for the sound of his breaths, though even that was muffled by the fog. Even the beat of the horse's hooves was muted, swallowed up in the white that swirled around them.

Hans brought them to a stop beside where Van Helsing stood. The older man glared at Karl as he climbed down from the cart.

'You're late.'

'Perhaps a little,' Karl smiled. 'But then I don't have an expensive gentleman's timepiece like yours, do I?'

He peered inquisitively at the watch in Van Helsing's hand. There was an inscription on the inside of the cover, he thought. Tatters of mist were drifting between the two men, though, and he only managed to make out the words, *With Love, Eliza,*

before Van Helsing snapped the cover shut and tucked the
watch back into the pocket of his waistcoat.

Hans fetched the tools from the cart and joined them, the
long-handled spades crossed over his shoulders, the strap of the
sack filled with the other items they would need slung across
his torso. Normally, the spades would be sufficient. Long gone
were the days of digging up the entire coffin to exhume a
corpse. It was swifter, easier, to take out the earth at the head-
end of the casket only, then prise back the lid until a
combination of hard muscle and the weight of the dirt at the
lower half of the coffin caused the wood to splinter and break.
Then the body could be dragged free, unless of course there was
a coffin collar in place, a loop of iron across the corpse's throat,
bolting it down to the floor of the coffin to thwart would-be
bodysnatchers. Karl had encountered the infernal things twice,
and both times his solution had been elegantly simple. He'd
placed the blade of the spade against the corpses' necks and put
his weight behind it, driving it through flesh and bone until the
head was severed. After that it was easy enough to drag the
dead out by their shoulders.

Crypts were different, though. A man couldn't dig his way
through stone, and there would be an iron gate or an oak door
to get past, chained and locked most likely. But there were
ways, Karl thought. There were always ways.

'Here.' The doctor opened his bag. 'Take these.'

He pulled out two strings of garlic cloves and handed them
to the men, then reached into the bag once more and withdrew
two simple wooden crosses.

Karl and Hans draped the strings around their necks, but as
he took his cross Karl found himself smiling. 'This is very sweet
of you. You want us to be safe?'

The doctor snapped his bag shut. 'I need you alive.' He
glanced up at the lightening sky. 'We should hurry.'

Karl shrugged, tucking the cross into his tunic, next to the gold. 'It's daylight. Legend says your quarry fears the sun.'

'My...quarry is not the only danger here,' the doctor said grimly. 'Quick now.'

He turned and moved into the graveyard, and a moment later, Karl and Hans followed.

They walked deeper into the necropolis. Twigs and dead leaves, almost invisible in the mist, crackled and snapped beneath their boots while above them, the tangled branches of trees bristled with rooks that watched their expedition with mournful indifference. Van Helsing led the way, navigating tombstones with speed and confidence, as if he'd made this journey a thousand times in his dreams. Some of the graves were family plots, Karl noticed, father and son sunk into the same soil decades apart. One of the markers caught his eye, not a headstone, but a simple wooden cross implanted into the earth, that of an infant, fallen prey to some mortal fever two days after its birth. Karl read the name scratched into the wood, the pitiful proximity of the dates that defined the child's life, and couldn't stop himself imagining the scattering of tiny bones turning to dust beneath his feet. A tear of cold sweat zigzagged down his ribcage, making him suppress a shudder.

At last they reached the crypt, a grey, moss-threaded edifice sunk into the side of a hill at the edge of the graveyard. The mist seemed thicker here, as if this were the source, as if the mist was the stone's cold breath. Beneath a vaulted roof supported by grooved columns, Karl could see the door, oak rather than iron, and the two heavy, rusting locks pressed into the wood, one at the top and one at the bottom. No chains, though.

Van Helsing hesitated, and Karl strode past him to pull at the door. The hinges rattled, but the door didn't move. He turned back to Van Helsing.

'You seem well prepared, Herr doctor,' he said. 'I don't

suppose that means you have a key?'

'It's locked from the inside,' Van Helsing told him. 'You'll need to—'

Karl held up a hand to silence him. 'Break the locks.' He smiled. 'Relax, Herr doctor. I know what to do.'

At a nod from Karl, Hans tossed the spades to the ground and reached into the bag. He pulled out a couple of iron crows, bars of strong metal the length of a man's forearm, their blunt ends hammered into hooks, perfect for prising open crates or caskets. Karl took the crows from his brother and worked one of them as deep as he could into the narrow space between the oak door and the stone that framed it. He placed it well, just above the topmost lock of the door, angled slightly downward. Hans passed him a mallet from the bag and Karl gave the jutting bar three or four good strikes, driving it deeper into the gap. The sound of each impact echoed in the dawn air like rifle shots, sending the rooks fleeing from their branches in a flock of beating wings and screeches of alarm. Karl repeated the process with the second bar, this one angled downwards towards the lowest of the locks, then stood back, wiping beads of sweat and chips of stone from his brow.

Hans stepped forward, his big hands grasping the lowest bar, his broad shoulders hunching as he pulled it sideways, prising the lock away from its moorings. Stone cracked around the mechanism and the bolts that held it. Hans pulled harder, the sweat steaming from his forehead, the thick cords of his neck taut with the effort. At last the lock sprang free, taking a slice of the door and a scattering of stone fragments with it as it tumbled to the earth.

From somewhere in the graveyard, from somewhere in the mist, something howled.

Hans paused, his hands already on the topmost bar, the muscles of his forearms tightening as he prepared to wrench the second lock from its anchor. He stared at Karl with wide eyes, the stump of his tongue reflexively darting out to wet arid lips. Karl turned away, seeking the source of the sound, but the wall of white mist swirled around them, all but impenetrable. The gravestones were little more than sketches in its shifting tides, the naked trees only the shadows of skeletons.

'He knows we're here,' Van Helsing said behind him.

Karl kept his eyes on the mist. 'Then we won't keep him waiting,' he said quietly. He knuckled a bead of sweat from his eye. 'Hurry, Hans.'

He heard his brother set to work on the second lock, heard the cracking of stone and the splintering of oak, and after a minute or so he heard the clatter of metal upon metal as the mechanism joined its twin on the soil.

He turned back to the crypt, and saw that Van Helsing was studying that damned pocket watch again. Hans, crimson-faced and sweating, had pulled the iron crow free of its space between oak and stone, and Karl saw that the door to the crypt was already swinging outward, only darkness beyond, and without thinking his hand darted from brow to belly and shoulder to shoulder. He thought perhaps the lack of conscious thought behind the gesture frightened him most of all. He hadn't made the sign of the cross since he was a boy.

He glanced across at Van Helsing and saw him snap his timepiece shut. The doctor raised his head, his thin lips parting to speak, but he froze, his blue eyes looking not at Karl but beyond him. Hans was looking that way too, his mouth working soundlessly.

Slowly, Karl turned, and saw the wolf that stood impossibly on the ground in front of him.

The raised spikes of its pelt were a ghostly white, almost as white as the mist that danced lazily around it, almost as though the animal's sleekly muscled form had materialised from the vapour itself. Karl would have known from its low, angled stance that it was preparing to attack, even without noting the splashes of colour in the whiteness; the scarlet tongue, rolled back behind crimson gums and long, sharp teeth, the wet smudge of its nose, sniffing for his fear, and the wild eyes that fixed him with a stare as black as the stitches between stars.

And somehow, impossibly, the beast was silent. The wrinkled folds of its muzzle told him that it was snarling, but no sound came from its mouth. The swell and ebb of its belly told him that it was breathing hard, and fast, but Karl couldn't hear it. Even when it took a cautious step forward, there was no crackling sigh from the twigs and leaves beneath its paw.

Karl could have forgiven himself for missing its approach. His mind had been distracted by that strange, somehow inquisitive emptiness that seemed to radiate from the darkness beyond the door, as if cold fingers were reaching into his brain to pick up and discard his every thought like a child with a roomful of toys. He could have forgiven himself, because the wolf had been born to hunt, had been spilled steaming from its mother's belly with its cunning and its instincts already ready to bloom. It was in the beast's nature to be dangerous and fast. Fast and quiet.

So, yes, he might not have heard the animal's stealthy advance, but the absolute silence that blanketed the wolf now was unnatural, was nothing less than sorcery.

Slowly, he unsheathed his hunting knife. From the corner of his eye he could see Hans shifting the iron bar in his hands, sliding it into a position where he might use it as a club. Behind Hans, Van Helsing had drawn a crucifix from his pocket, silver and finely sculpted rather than the crude wooden versions he'd given to Karl and his brother.

'That won't help you, Herr doctor.' Karl whispered. His palm sweated around the handle of the knife. 'This is not your devil from the crypt.'

Van Helsing's voice was steady. 'No. It is his protector.'

'His—' Karl turned back to the doctor, a question on his

lips, and in the heartbeat that his gaze left the wolf, the animal leapt. Karl whipped his head back in the beast's direction, already bringing the hunting knife up to defend himself, but he knew those teeth would reach his face before he could raise the blade high enough to bury it in muscle and fur.

The wolf was a white blur of movement, but suddenly Karl became aware that there was another movement behind him, and of a blunt, thudding pain between his shoulderblades. The hunting knife flew from his hand. Then the earth was falling away beneath him, or rather, he was rising, his boots leaving the soil in a scatter of twigs and leaves. He cried out in surprise and pain at the impact to his back, and before the cry was done he was back on the ground, rolling in the graveyard dirt, the breath stolen from his lungs.

Hans stood over him, the iron crow in his hands. His brother had shoved him out of the creature's path, taken Karl's place, and was sweeping the iron crow in a wide arc, meaning to cleave the wolf's skull in two. He misjudged the swing though, and as the metal bar swept harmlessly above its head the creature clamped its jaws around Hans' throat.

Hans stumbled backwards, losing his grip on the metal bar. His hands sank into the wolf's fur, trying to pry the animal loose, but the teeth were hooked into the stubbled meat of his neck, the muzzle half-buried beneath his jaw. Around the struggle, the clouds of mist ran red.

'No!' Karl tried to scream, but his lungs were empty. Hans was screaming, though, strange, liquid cries that sang up into the white sky. With every shriek, the ragged flap of his tongue jerked from his mouth. Karl hadn't heard his brother scream since their father had taken to his eldest boy with his hunting knife, and he remembered how those cries had abruptly transformed into choked, bubbling grunts as the flesh had been severed. Panicked and terrified, Karl had pressed a rough blanket to the injury until the bleeding ceased, and then used

what little mending skills his mother had taught him to stitch
the frayed edges of the wound together. But that had been
later, after Karl had taken his own knife and made sure their
father's screams had been sweet and clear right up until the
moment that Karl had slit his throat.

Now he saw Hans stagger and fall, and still the wolf clung
to him. His fists beat at the beast's hide, but Karl noted with
horror that the blows were growing weaker. His cries were
dwindling too, becoming more like those strangled grunts of
his boyhood. As Hans' shrieks lessened, Karl could hear how,
even in the frenzy of attack, there was still no sound from the
wolf's throat. Save for the wet tearing sounds of its teeth and
the scrape of its claws on the leather of Hans' tunic, the animal
was utterly silent.

Karl struggled to get to his feet, but Van Helsing was
already springing forward, raising his silver crucifix above his
head. The leap was ungainly, the doctor all spidery, bony angles
but his eyes were focussed and hard, and in them Karl saw
something of the warrior against evil that the firelit tales spoke
of. Not that it would do him any good against the wolf, Karl
thought. The crucifix was a light, insubstantial weapon against
such a beast, something that would barely scratch the animal's
hide.

But then Van Helsing was raising the cross higher, and Karl
saw that the shape's lower half had been fashioned into a long,
thin blade, steel sprouting from silver. The doctor brought the
weapon down, planting it up to the crossbar in the thick mane
of fur at the base of the wolf's skull.

To Karl, the animal's agonised howl was as the sweetest
music.

Its jaws unlocked as it snapped its head back, letting Hans—
his poor, broken brother—slump back into the soil. The wolf
arched its back, twisting its head around as if it were trying to
sink its teeth into whatever was causing it such pain. Van

Helsing had let go of the crucifix, though, and was retreating, his face as pale as mushrooms, his blue eyes wild. The wolf leapt from Hans' chest and spun in anguished circles, snapping and snarling, thrashing its head from side to side, seeking to dislodge the blade. Thin sunlight reflected from the cross's polished planes, almost as if it were on fire.

The cross *was* on fire.

No, not the cross. There were flames, yes, but they were leaping *from* the silvery shape rather than engulfing it, spreading along the coarse hide of the wolf, crisping its fur, turning white to black. Curls of greasy smoke were unwinding from the muzzle, stinking like overcooked meat, and Karl realised that the strange flames were consuming the animal from without and from within. It hopped and leaped and howled as its paws caught fire, then sprang away from the men, running off into the mist.

Its outline of fire and smoke burned in the distance for a moment before the white fog finally enveloped it, and a moment later its howls and yelps dwindled into silence.

'Hans.' Karl half-ran, half-stumbled to where his brother lay, unmoving. He sank to his knees beside him, something akin to that terrible childhood panic gnawing at his senses. 'Hans,' he said again, though the lightless orbs of his brother's eyes, the tangle of wet rags that was all that remained of his throat, told him that there would be no answer.

'No,' he muttered, bowing his head. He swallowed hard, his tongue bitter with tears. He took his brother's hand. 'No.'

He wanted to scream at the sky, to strike the earth with his fists, to be the one lying dead on the ground. His eyes burned. 'No.' It seemed as if that was all he could say.

Slowly, Van Helsing approached. He squatted down beside Hans and gently pressed his fingers to the dead man's wrist, nothing more than a formality, or a habit.

'I'm sorry,' he said.

Karl shook his head. He stared into Han's eyes, saw the fear of his last moments, and felt his heart break.

'We should get him inside,' he heard Van Helsing say. 'There may be more of those creatures.'

'And what if there are?' Karl said quietly. 'He's already dead.'

'They'll ...' The doctor hesitated. 'They'll salvage what remains of him. Desecrate his body. You can't—'

'You don't care about that.' Karl glared at him, his eyes red-rimmed and accusing. 'We are nothing more than beasts of burden to you. Beasts of burden or cannon fodder. You don't care. You just want to get into your damned crypt.'

'No, I ...' Van Helsing shook his head. He stared into the blackness beyond the doorway. 'There is a great power in there, something I must ...' His voice trailed off. 'Stay with him if you wish. I will help you take him back to the cart when I'm done here.' He rose, and crossed to retrieve his leather bag from where he'd discarded it.

'No,' Karl said. He reached down to close his brother's eyes, and stood. 'I am more than just your workhorse, Herr doctor, and so was Hans. *I* will carry him home, and *I* will tell his wife and children. We will bury him and mourn him together. But now...' He motioned towards the crypt. 'Now we go in there.'

Van Helsing frowned. 'But I thought—'

'The wolf,' Karl said. 'That was a servant of whatever hellspawn is in there, yes?'

Van Helsing nodded.

'Then it's decided.' Karl strode forward, past the doctor, and knelt at the sack of tools that Hans had carried from the cart. He tugged the bag open, drawing out an oil lantern.

'We will face the devil together,' he said. 'And when the moment comes to end its unholy life, I will be the one to drive a stake through its black heart.'

Beyond the door, a small flight of steps led down into an

arched corridor. The echo of their footsteps followed them as they advanced, their shadows dancing upon the curved walls in the orange glow of the lantern, sometimes leaping ahead of the two men, sometimes skulking behind, as if they feared what lay ahead. It was a few minutes before they came to another archway, this one opening up onto a wide, low-ceilinged chamber, empty but for the long, narrow plinth that sprouted from the stone floor, and upon that, the hard angles of a coffin glimmering in the lantern light.

Karl lifted the lantern a little higher, seeing that the wood was good, strong, engraved with a dozen strange symbols and dusted with a dark powder like soot. Some of the carved markings were worn at the edges, he saw, and the loops of iron bolted to the sides were scratched and tarnished, as though the casket had seen many burials over many centuries.

Van Helsing was tracing the edge of the lid with his fingers, his hand shaking slightly, his eyes wide, as though he couldn't quite believe that he was so close to his quarry.

'It's locked from the inside?' Karl asked him. 'Like the doors?'

'I don't think so,' the doctor said softly. 'From what I was told, the lid is easily removed, in case some calamity should occur. He wouldn't want to compromise his chances of escape. Help me.'

He placed his palms beneath the edge of the coffin lid, and began to push. The lid shifted, but only a little. Karl set the lantern down and moved to help him, and together they managed to slide the covering aside.

Inch by inch, the vampire's face was revealed. Karl had expected something that barely touched on human, some unnatural collision of man and bat, a nightmare of leathery flesh and fangs. But the face of the figure in the coffin, though pale and gaunt even in the warm glow of the lantern light, belonged not to a nightmare but to some lord of noble blood.

Thick black hair was swept back from a high forehead and
hawk-like features, and even his clothes, or as much as Karl
could see of them, looked to be made of the finest silks and
cottons. For a moment he thought that Van Helsing had led
them to the wrong coffin, that the creature's lair was elsewhere
in the crypt, until the lid slid down a little further, exposing the
chest, and he saw its steady rise and fall, one undead breath
after another.

'Van Helsing,' he whispered. 'Give me the stake.'

'What?' The doctor had been staring into the coffin, his
eyes distant, and now he blinked at Karl as if roused from a
trance, or a memory.

'The stake.' Karl said again. He reached out across the
coffin, his hand open. 'We must do what we came here to do.'

'Yes,' Van Helsing said. He opened his bag and reached
inside. 'Yes, of course.'

Karl had a moment to register that the doctor had
withdrawn not a stake but a pistol from the bag, before the
other man fired two shots that cracked thunderously in the
confined space, the echoes rolling back and forth between the
stone walls as the bullets tore into Karl's belly.

He felt a great *sucking* sensation in his middle as he
staggered back, as if his innards were all rushing to the same
space, and suddenly he was lying on the cold stone floor, his
hands at his guts, his guts in his hands. Blood gushed through
his fingers, shockingly warm.

'You should have taken my offer to wait outside,' the doctor
said, his voice winding through the echoes of the gunshots. 'You
might have lived another ten minutes.'

What are you doing? Karl tried to say, but his mouth was
flooding, and all he could manage was a thick, coppery gasp.
The weight in his hands grew heavier.

'He tracked me down, you see,' the doctor was saying. He
tucked the pistol into the pocket of his overcoat. 'I thought I'd

hidden myself well, but of course, seeking me out was nothing to the great hunter.'

'I don't ...' Karl coughed, feeling something tear inside him. He thought perhaps the lantern was burning up the last of its oil. All around him, the crypt was growing darker. 'I don't understand.'

'He came to me to ask for my help,' the older man smiled. 'Said that we were both men of learning, of science. He implored me to join him, so that together we might do God's work.'

He laughed softly, once more reaching into the bag. The gold inscription on the leather glittered in the lantern light. 'If only he had known. My own work has already left God's labours far behind.'

'But you...*you* are the hunter.' Karl wheezed. '*You* are Van Helsing.'

'Van Helsing is dead,' the doctor said, raising the object he'd drawn from the leather bag. The last of the lantern's flame burned dully on the bone-saw's steel teeth. 'My name is Victor Frankenstein.' He smiled at the figure in the coffin. 'And my monster needs a brain.'

Cthulhu Doesn't Dance

ALISON CYBE

"All the world's a stage,
And all the men and women merely players"
William Shakespeare

The stars were definitely not right, not even close–in fact, the paint on them was still wet. I looked at the backdrop, and tried to piece together just what it was that didn't look right. I couldn't complain about the paint still being wet, Sam had been working on the set design for the play flat-out for the last week, and building an entire royal chamber on the boundary of a lake on an alien planet was bound to be a challenge. I counted the suns; there were two. That was correct. I checked the moon–Sam had complained about the moon endlessly, stating categorically that it should not sit both behind and in front of the towers on the opposite shore of the lake. I had reassured him, telling him confidently that this was what the play required. Now, though, I honestly just wanted the entire performance to be over.

"The stars are white!" I snapped, realising what was wrong. "They're supposed to be black."

Sam looked at me with the weary, worn-down expression of a much put-upon set designer, the kind of expression that only a veteran of his field can manage. "That makes no sense," he stated matter-of-factly. "Black stars against a night sky? How are the audience supposed to see them?"

For the sixth time that day, I wanted to crawl into a bottle of cheap whisky and forget the day. "I don't know. I don't know, just...just paint them black, okay?"

I realised that I was snapping. I was quite well aware that my nerves were on edge, that I was frayed to the edge. We had less than two days left of rehearsals, and at the pace we were achieving, *The King in Yellow* was going to be the biggest turkey to hit the west end.

Last night, Malcolm Emmery had sat with me in the bed-and-breakfast room that I had rented for the duration of the performance, and told me that he was ditching the performance.

"Richard," he had said, "I'm sorry to leave you at the eleventh hour. But let's be bluntly honest, hun. This entire play, it simply isn't going to fly."

"Your lack of faith is astonishing," I had admonished him. "Is this about the leading man?"

"My dear," he said, in that Grande Dame affected style of his, lightly brushing a few stray flecks of pipe-ash from his tweed sleeve, "You and I both know that he simply doesn't have anything going for him except for a very pretty face. Our young Will is like a deer stuck in a pair of headlights; lovely to look at, but liable to just stand there and freeze if he gets scared."

"This isn't about William," I had chided him, "This is about that soppy young tart you've had strapped to your arm for the last three weeks."

"I'll thank you not to speak about him in that way!" snorted Malcolm. "But no, seeing as you ask quite so eloquently, I'll confess that I don't entirely trust our backer."

I couldn't help but agree with Malcolm on this point. The

play was being funded in its entirety by an elderly gentleman known only as Alfred Senworth. His name was entirely unknown to myself or to Malcolm, nor to any other contact I had made both in Broadway and the London stage (a perilously small cadre of contacts, sadly). The man had deigned to visit us only once, during our casting sessions, to provide us with a neatly typed document that comprised of the script and stage notes for *The King in Yellow*. Mr Senworth was a man who appeared to be well into his eighties, and walked hunched over a stick whilst chuckling in amusement to himself. Since that one very fleeting glimpse, we had seen neither hide nor hair of the benefactor, although curiously he paid us considerably to manage the performance in his stead; and paid us handsomely, at that! The man seemed to possess a near-unlimited source of income, which he gladly passed along to us in order to give his dream form.

Malcolm took a puff of his pipe. "I'm sorry, Richard. Quite frankly, the entire thing gives me the willies."

"Come now!" I had sighed. "He's just some harmless old quack. We put on the performance for him, and it'll be the easiest job we've ever had."

"Did you know that it's cursed?" he asked me.

If I had been drinking (and by this point in the production, that was quickly becoming my favourite way to pass the evenings), I would have spat my mouthful across my friend's lap. "Don't be ridiculous. You're an intelligent man, Malcolm. We've had a few hiccups in production, but to say that it's cursed? That's patently absurd!"

He shook his head. "I'm not talking about the hiccups. Although they may play a part in this as well, Richard. If they do, I'd bet that they're only going to get worse. I'm sorry, my friend. You know that I respect you, but I just have to count myself out of this one." As he rose to leave, he turned to me and smiled. "Besides, I think you know as well as I do, this turkey isn't going to fly."

And that was how I wound up producing this entire production on my own. From that point on, the hiccups had grown into roadblocks. Then they had become mountains.

"You, sir, should unmask!" announced Camilla.

Standing downstage and slightly to her right, the Stranger made a subtle movement with his hand, as if to embrace his face. I made a note; I'd need to talk to him about that. "Indeed?" he asked.

Camilla continued. "Indeed, it's time." God, her performance was about as lively as a corpse. An especially dead one, perhaps one that was still locked in a box somewhere. Camilla delivered her next lines as if each one had a lead weight tied to it, "We have all laid aside disguise but you."

The Stranger raised his arms, and announced, "I wear no mask!"

"No mask?" quailed Camilla, "No mask!"

Then the Stranger's mask fell off.

It struck the stage floor with a thud, and Camilla almost stamped her foot. "That's it!" she declared, "That is absolutely it! I have never, in all my days, been part of such an amateurish performance!"

As she strode offstage towards the dressing room, Will picked up the broken pieces of the mask. Playing the Stranger, Will had perilously few lines, and given his utter inability to recall any of them on demand, that was distinctly for the best. "Did I do something wrong?" he asked.

I shook my head, stepping up onto the stage. "No, you were fine," I reassured him, taking the mask. I looked it over; it was pallid enough, but now it was also split into two large chunks. I made a mental note to check the script to see if it said anything about the mask being cracked–perhaps it might look more dramatic that way. "Okay," I called, "whilst our leading lady cools her heels, let's go over Cassilda's song, and the arrival of the King. Where's Amber and Mark?"

I found the two of them in the costume room, smoking a joint and chuckling at Mark's artwork. After almost half an hour's worth of delay and repeated reminders that the opening night was tomorrow evening, I marched them both up onstage.

The two had, sadly, come as a pair. Amber was one of the best vocalists who had attended the casting sessions. Her voice was magnificent. Her only request in order to confirm her role, however, was that we extend a similar role to her boyfriend, Mark. Mark was an artist, and a self-styled free-thinker. He walked barefoot onto the stage with a perpetual scent of weed hanging from his clothing. His first words upon meeting me were, "Groovy theatre you own here, dude. So, I'm playing some kind of king, yeah?" I didn't have the heart to tell him that we were only renting the theatre.

As they got into costume, I took a moment to flick through Mark's sketchbook, which he had left sitting near the front of the stage. When I found his fifth nude pencil drawing of Amber, this one with her thighs spread wide to accept the body of a well-endowed satyr whose facial features bore an uncanny resemblance to Mark, I stopped and wished I hadn't ventured a look in the first place.

As Amber took centre stage, Mark stumbled back to slouch down beside me, stumbling over his costume's yellow tattered robes as he did so. "Dude," he began, "I think I lost my lantern."

Cassilda began her aria. Her voice was, as ever, stunning.

"Did you hear me?" asked Mark.

I shushed him. "I'll get you another one before tomorrow."

"Bitchin'," he replied. Yes, I thought, quite.

Cassilda continued into her next verse. She sang of Carcosa, her lost home. She sings of the beauty, its black stars (Sam was working hurriedly on those), its cloudy shores.

Mark turned to me. "So, like, Amber's playing Camilla, right?"

I sighed, "No. She's playing Cassilda."

"Oh!" said Mark, as if everything had suddenly made sense. Then he asked, "What's the difference?"

"Camilla's the daughter" I explained, wearily.

"Oh!" said Mark, again, as if he had just discovered the solution to turning lead into gold. Another few seconds passed, and then he asked, "And they're from Carcoda?"

"Carcosa," I explained.

"That's totally confusing," he grumbled. "Having so many characters that all start with the same letter. Totally lame."

I ignored him, and focused on Amber's singing. She caught the notes perfectly, encapsulating each one with such sadness, such longing. She continued, "Songs that the Hyades shall sing, where flaps the tatters of the King."

Mark beamed, and nudged me. "That's me," he said. "The king." I resisted the urge to smack him upside the head with my copy of the script. "What's a hidies?"

I exhaled slowly. "The Hyades are stars. In the play, we were going to represent them as a trio of women, like a chorus."

"Where are they?" he asked.

"Two of them broke their ankles last week when the curtain fell on them," I grumbled, having worked so hard to forget that episode. "Now we only have one left."

Mark nodded. I returned my attention to the stage, for a few seconds.

I was anticipating his next outburst. "Hey!" he yelled, excitedly, "Why's this the only musical number in the show?"

God, I'd have happily killed the man for a strong bottle of whisky. Actually, I'd have happily killed him, after having put up with this kind of nonsense for three weeks.

Calmly, with very patient breaths, I said, "It's not a musical number. It's an aria. There's a difference."

My explanation fell on deaf ears. "We should, like, totally have more musical numbers. I could do one. I mean, I'm playing the title character, aren't I? I should really have a musical number!"

I started to rub my forehead. On the stage, Amber's song finished.

"Like, what was that other character from those old stories?" Mark continued, wracking his brain. "Cthulhu! Yeah, he should guest star in this story!"

I shook my head, "No. No, the legend of Hastur and the King in Yellow weren't made by Lovecraft, they were older. This play is older. It wouldn't fit. None of it would..."

Mark began to pat my shoulders, rubbing them back and forth in that way that always annoyed me. "No, really, dude!" he said, as if that were a convincing case in and of itself. "Let's give it a shot. Look, give me one evening, I can have a musical number ready. My cousin Jimmy, he plays guitar, he could do us an awesome backing track. We could have Cthulhu show up in the play and do a whole musical number!"

I was biting down on the inside of my cheek so hard that I could swear I could taste copper. "The play opens tomorrow!" I repeated.

"Dude, don't worry!" explained Mark. "It'll be ready to go in time. It'll be a blast. We can even have the guy, Cthulhu, do an awesome dance number for it. Something really smooth, like greased lightning. Man, I'm stoked for this, I really am!"

I sunk down into the chair, and started to sob. "No. No, just... just no. Cthulhu doesn't dance!"

Naturally, Mark stormed out when I wouldn't give him his musical number, taking Amber with him. At that point, I retired to my room and tried to swallow as much Jack Daniels as a human being could manage.

That night, I had a nightmare. A large, towering figure

wrapped entirely in tattered yellow robes peeled his way from the ceiling of my bed-and-breakfast room, determined to absorb my very soul.

I awoke the next morning with only twelve hours before our first performance and a headache that could have killed a bull elephant, and frankly I would rather have stuck with the nightmare.

With less than an hour before the curtain rose, the actress who was playing Camilla had decided to throw another temper tantrum. "This is intolerable!" she declared, marching back and forth with the type of confidence that was normally only reserved for heavily armed marines. "Utterly intolerable! I will not–I repeat, not–share my dressing room with that...that understudy! This won't do, do you hear me?" she shouted, jamming her finger roughly in my direction.

Megan was, to put it bluntly, untalented. Not only for the role of Camilla, who she managed to capture with all of the charisma of an especially overcooked lump of beef, but potentially untalented for any role in any play. Nevertheless, she had appeared in four of them, and as a result had more on-stage experience than the rest of the acting cast, all of who were busying themselves by getting into costume.

"Megan," I pleaded as I tried to quickly finish moving the set into place on the stage, "darling. Please, Amber has left the production. We have nobody else to fill her role except for her understudy!"

She snapped her fingers, "I am not some lowly amateur performer, my dear man!" Oh god, I knew what was coming next. It was the same speech that she had performed yesterday. And on Monday. And four times last week. "I'll have you know that I was Lady Macbeth! The *Times* called my performance 'invigorating.' And now you expect me to get changed amongst the rest of these...these proles?"

I really wanted to tell her exactly what I thought. Every inch of me was screaming to do just that. But when I glanced at my watch (forty-two minutes until curtain), I knew that I simply couldn't risk losing another one of the cast. "Yes," I sighed, trying to ignore the pounding ache in my skull, "You're absolutely right. You can use my office. But please, can you be quick?" I leaned down to pick up a large, foam deco pillar that would form the doorway into the royal chambers. The paint on it was, I realised only far too late, still wet.

"I should hope so!" continued Megan, flipping her hair back and forth in what I could only assume was an attempt to make herself look big. "Now, I'll need a bottle of spring water. That's still water, not fizzy. Oh my god, it had better not be fizzy water, I can tell you that. And it has to be naturally distilled..."

I tuned her out while I attempted to scrub the paint from my hands, wiping them frantically on my trousers. That was when I caught sight of a figure–short, hunched, dark, the figure shuffled through the bustling crowds towards me. As he drew closer, I realised that it was Alfred, and not in fact some kind of horrible goblin. The old man stopped before me and forced his aged face into a smile. "Richard, my dear young man," he spoke through a raspy voice.

He extended a gnarled talon of a hand to me. I dropped the piece of scenery, and hurriedly wiped the remnants of the paint on my jeans. "Oh, Mister Senworth. I didn't expect to see you here!" I exclaimed.

"Excuse me?" interjected Megan.

"Pah, not at all," explained Alfred. "How could I resist having a little peek backstage before the performance?"

I smiled, nervously. The man was, after all, paying my wage. "I hope that it's all to your liking."

He nodded, "Me and my friends can't wait for the performance. I tell you, my boy, it's going to be a resounding success!"

"Excuse me?" repeated Megan, growing quite irritated that my attention had been diverted elsewhere. "Hello?"

I motioned to her to give me just a moment. "Will you be watching as well?"

"My boy, I have a box already set aside. The theatre is bustling, I tell you. I haven't quite seen so many like-minded and eager fans since, oh, since the last time the stars were right!" he said, his voice positively glowing with excitement.

"Richard!" snapped Megan, "Let me tell you, that understudy, she's utterly incompetent!"

"Yes, yes." I nodded to her, trying to keep her quiet.

Alfred flexed his fingers together, and said something that I could barely understand over Megan's complaints. "Why," he whispered, "it wouldn't surprise me if Hastur himself were to come down to watch the performance in person."

I smiled to him, and was just about to reply, when Megan grabbed my shoulder and whispered harshly into my ear, "I don't think that she's even a member of equity!"

"Megan!" I snapped back, and pulled her to one side.

"Yes," continued Alfred, "I think that this performance should be quite ideal. It summons him, don't you know? The avatar of Hastur, the ancient one. The play is a spell; its performance, the ritual. I have invited all of my colleagues, my associates, every member of the cult of Hastur, to be in attendance at this theatre this evening. We shall bring Hastur down from the stars and onto the earth–here, to London. Won't it be marvellous?"

"Yes," I said, not really listening to a word he said. "Marvellous. Wonderful. Look, Megan, the performance begins in less than forty-five minutes. Will you please get in costume?"

Giving me a look that could have killed a weaker man, Megan snorted. "Very well. But I tell you, I don't even think that understudy is even British!"

I was already walking back over to Alfred. "Yes, yes," I said to her.

"And if Immigration charges in during the performance and cart her away," said Megan, finally, "don't say that I didn't warn you!"

On the whole, the performance could have gone far, far worse.

The first scene of Act one passed without any major concerns. Always the most placid and simple of the scenes, the first act contained little more than Cassilda reclining on the shores of Lake Hali, in the mysterious kingdom of Yhtill. She received three messengers: her two sons, and her daughter Camilla. Each brings her news of the impending arrival of The Stranger, a masked figure who has travelled to her court from the distant lands of Aldebaran, bearing a message of warning concerning the King in Yellow. Frankly, the entire storyline of the play made little sense to me, but who was I to doubt the works of the playwright, whoever he may have been.

When presented with the news from her children of The Stranger's coming, Cassilda was wistful and uninterested, instead mourning the loss of her kingdom's magnificence and beauty. The audience also seemed wistful and uninterested, and several yawned their way through the entire act. The only moment that seemed especially grating, though, was when Cassilda stated quite matter-of-factly that she did not fear the coming of the Stranger, or of the King; she only feared the Yellow Sign, a peculiar symbol that had a terrifying effect upon her. When, not two minutes later, the Stranger marched onstage with the Yellow Sign painted sloppily over his frock, one member of the audience shouted out "Oi, what a dick move!"

At this point, things were going quite alright. Mark's understudy had no lines of dialogue, and so the Stranger that he played had only to stand there and wear a pallid mask, which I had hurriedly set back together with super-glue. We were now into the second act, which meant that Cassilda was to sing her aria, a moving song explaining her sense of loss of her childhood homeland of Carcosa. Two minutes into her song, three police officers pushed their way onstage and removed Cassilda from the performance under suspicion of being an illegal immigrant.

I quickly called the cast and crew together, and put together a new plan. We would start the second act now, placing the unmasking of the Stranger at the start of the act. We had, however, no actors remaining to play the King in Yellow, so I explained that as the role required no dialogue, I would put on the tattered robes and play the part myself. Cassilda, who had already given the majority of her performance, would be played by the single remaining Hyades – the one who had not broken her ankle some days prior.

Fifteen minutes later, and the royal ball proceeded quite smoothly. Camilla delivered her line to the Stranger, "You, sir, should unmask."

"Indeed?" replied the Stranger.

"Indeed, it's time," said Cassilda, whose voice sounded entirely different and was six inches shorter than she had been in the previous act, "We all have laid aside our disguises but you."

The Stranger threw up his arms, and announced, "I wear no mask!" His arm knocked one of the foam deco pillars, which collapsed onto one of the dancing guests. Two extras hurried to help the dazed man off the stage.

Camilla turned towards the audience, which I had told her specifically not to do, and screamed "No mask? No mask!"

And of course, the elastic on the mask snapped at that point, causing it to fall off.

By this point, all I could do was think about how much I was getting paid for this. Malcolm was right; this turkey was definitely not flying. I pulled on the tattered yellow robe, and hurried into position. The plan from here to the end of the play was simple–I, as the King in Yellow, strode onto the stage from the left and, with a terrifying darkness, was to hold the ballroom to my sway. I would hold forth the masks, which the assembled cast donned, only for them to fall and writhe on the floor. The King then walks through the congregation, gathering those who would serve him, and taking them to war with Aldeberan, which by that point glows as a giant haunting red colour on the backdrop.

I pulled the tattered hood up to obscure my face, and waited for the line. Not long thereafter, it came–Cassilda called out, "Not upon us, O King, not upon us!" I made to step out onto the stage–

When another, taller figure swept past me. He strode out onto the stage, his flapping tatters bristling as he moved.

I stopped, watching the figure. He was far taller than a normal man, but with his back turned to me, I had no idea who he might have been. I lowered my hood, staring in bewilderment.

It was about at that time that two of the stage lights burst. The sparks from one of them caught onto the painted backdrop, which promptly collapsed in a heap of burning mass. By the time the fire had spread to the curtains, the audience were already running for their lives. Frankly, this came as something of a relief, if I'm entirely honest.

Malcolm would later tell me that the cost of refurbishing the theatre brought our net profit for the production into negative numbers. He also took great pleasure in pointing out that we received relatively few negative reviews–although it was true that several of the critics in attendance were later institutionalised when they fell into a trance-like state, screaming "The eyes! The eyes!" But aside from those minor hitches, and the theatre burning down, and the pending lawsuits, and the pending investigations by the police–on the whole, the production went significantly better than I thought it would!

It's just as Malcolm had always said–that's show business.

Suicide Solution

ROB TEUN

Quinn could not contain his excitement; he was hoping to die tonight.

Immense black trees surrounded the clearing around the lake where Quinn stood.

"From ashes to ashes, from dust to dust. Really, what is the Divine's plan? Living, dying, and fucking people we soon grow bored of fucking. More lives to watch and forget than remember. I will tell who he is. God is not some infinitely wise being with a long beard in the clouds so high you cannot see him. He is nothing but a kid with an ant farm who got bored of watching them whittle away the hours with work and sleep. In the end, how can it all matter? There's no fucking heaven for us, not even a hell," said a voice.

Quinn turned and faced the man known only as Maker, a man as thin as air. His pale skin luminous in the light of the moon.

"Will this be it, the end? The big finish?" asked Quinn.

"Don't look so worried."

This was it, now and forever, with no turning back.

"You're the one who is going to kill me," said Maker.

"No, no, no, this is fucked up. You're here to kill me so I can live forever."

A cold heavy stake dropped into Quinn's palms.

Maker reached out, grabbed hold of Quinn's wrists, and impaled himself onto the stake. Quinn tried to pull away, but

Maker pushed himself harder onto the point until it felt like it touched his spine.

Maker looked Quinn in the eye with a bloodied smile before his body slumped to the floor like a broken toy.

Quinn loomed over the mentor who never taught him enough.

An ocean of blue light washed over the stars, a wail of police sirens howled at the moon; tires tore into the grass as they pulled to a stop. A click of the car door, a cocking of a gun.

"Put your hands up and drop your weapon!" screamed a voice from behind Quinn.

Measured footfalls creeping up from behind him. Quinn let the bloodied stake slip, held up his hands, not resisting the steel cuffs as they snapped around his wrists.

"Hey, Alan! Come and throw this fucking psycho in the back of the car. Don't worry about his head when you duck him in the back." Cruel laughter echoed in Quinn's ears.

Quinn concluded that Maker called the cops to his murder: how else could they have known or made it here so quick? If Maker was to be dead to the world, why did it have to be like this?

"Hey Alan, it's only nine o'clock and the whack-a-do's are out already!"

Alan and Frank readied themselves for the play-ahead upon the stage of the interview room. The fingerprint smudges of thousands of criminals pressed into immortality on the steel interview table.

Frank and Alan are as different as night and day stood together. Frank was a short but powerfully built man, a heavy head with a craggy face carved from contempt. Alan had softer features but stood taller. His skin an ill-fitting hood stretched over his face.

"So what do you think we have here? A fuckin' mime?" said Frank as he handed Alan a Chesterfield brand cigarette. "I'm gettin' angry askin' the same question a second time."

"What Detective Malone means to say is that's its better all round that you just cooperate, so I'm not going to call you John Doe all night, so tell me, what's your name? I'm Detective Alan Smith."

For the first time that night, Quinn smiled.

"You got caught. It's all fun and fuckin' games till you get caught. But now we gotcha. Okay, mister mystery, you've just made the big time. Now, we're gonna have a little Q and A, and at the risk of sounding redundant, please make your answers genuine," said Frank.

"Isn't this where you're supposed to lull me into a false sense of security? Isn't this where you're supposed to convince me that you're my friend?" said Quinn.

Frank slammed his meaty hand onto the table; the metal vibrated and echoed painfully around the interview room. Alan flinched; he had felt that fist before. "I ain't your friend. I'm the Anti-Christ. You get me in a vendetta kind of mood. Now, we got you at the crime scene with a stake in the poor bastard's chest. What did he do to you? Was it revenge? Did he fuck your wife? Did he rob you?"

Quinn continued to smile, that strange all-knowing little grin.

"Alan. Take over for a moment," Frank said between his gritted teeth, bringing his coffee to his lips before taking a seat against the wall.

"So what is your name? You could be innocent and if you are then tell us your name. You've nothing to lose by telling us," asked Alan.

"My name's Quinn."

"Finally we're getting somewhere," Frank looked at his watch as he spoke. It read 9:45 pm. Its digital glow a blur within the sea of the overhead strip light.

Before Frank could continue, a knock came from the door. Frank strained his bulky frame out of his chair to answer the door. Quinn saw Frank's lips move, yet heard nothing. He was more interested in what the person behind the door was saying. Frank uttered a few words, unheard by those in the interview room. Shutting the door behind him, Frank fell against the door and pulled deeply on his cigarette, blowing the blue smoke towards the ceiling.

Alan looked onward at Frank.

"What's the latest, Frank?"

Quinn peered down at his hands beneath the table. His nails had grown into short spearheads sharp enough to cut the throat of God. Maker had told him this would happen in time, among other changes. Some blessings and others curses.

"Hey, boy, look at me," said Frank.

Quinn looked up at Frank, breath held.

"Finally sinking in, is it? Shame that. They'll love you in prison. Got bitch wrote all over you."

"Wha—"

"Shut up. I got news for you...you're not a killer. Not yet anyway," replied Frank.

Quinn opened his mouth then shut it again. His teeth felt bigger in his mouth. At some point, they had grown since he had entered the room. Running his tongue over and along them confirmed it.

"What's going on, Frank?" asked Alan.

"How can I put this? The body, the victim, was on the slab ready to go. The coroner left the room because he needed something, a fuckin' sandwich knowing that sack of fat. When he got back, the body was gone. Just like that, he had gone as if he was never there." Frank looked as though he was still trying to process everything.

Alan's brow furrowed, "So any whereabouts on where this

guy has gone? What the hell is going on?"

Frank's fingers gripped into Quinn's shoulder.

"Don't think for one second you're getting away with this. People like you make me sick. Even if he does turn up alive, you are still looking at an attempted murder charge. There will be a body somewhere. So don't look so damn happy."

"Hey Frank, fancy some coffee?" said Alan, stepping forward to intervene.

"Fuck the coffee Alan, look at this freak," said Frank as he reached over and took hold of Quinn's hand, turning it palm facing down. "Who does he think he is? That shit-eating grin. The way he thinks that nearly killing a man is okay. I see fuckheads like this all day, every day. They make me sick." Spittle ran down the corner of Frank's mouth.

"I'm getting some coffee," said Alan. "I don't want any part of this."

Quinn looked upwards at Frank, brought his hands from beneath the table and placed them on the surface, his nails scraping against the metal.

"We're not so different me and you. We both have secrets, things to hide," said Quinn.

Frank stepped back with his arms across his chest as though he had to hold his secrets in.

He no longer had a wife to go home to; she had left him some years ago. The final straw for Annette came when she found the extra money came from the old Chinese man who was left with broken fingers for not coughing up the protection cash, the prostitute left for dead after Frank "kept her in line" just that one time too many.

"The greatest trick the devil ever performed was to convince the world he did not exist...So when you go home, what is it your wife sees when you get home? Does she see a fat corrupt cop? Or her husband?"

Quinn recoiled as Frank bolted forward, his hands

wrapping around Quinn's face, Quinn's hands meeting Frank's with a strength he did not know he possessed. Quinn's nails dug into the skin of Frank's hands. Quinn watched Frank pull his hands away; his skin pulled taut as if caught on a rusty nail. Frank yanked away and held up his hands in front of him, the skin opened cleanly where the razor like nails had slashed. Frank tore at his shirt not caring how it looked. He quickly wrapped his hands in the shirt to stop the bloodflow.

"You mother—" Frank shook his head. "You're going to pay for that!" screeched Frank, his head leering forward.

At that same moment, Alan entered, rushing the few steps needed to reach his partner.

Quinn sat there with all the innocence of a child. The serene look on his face unsettled Alan. Frank continued to scream obscenities around the room while clutching the shirt that covered his hands. The once crisp white shirt was now a sopping red mess.

"What the fuck is going on?" asked Alan as he cupped Frank's hands to see the extent of the damage.

Before he could lift the shirt away from Frank's hands, Frank was already in front of Quinn, his hands fumbling to get a grip on Quinn's face. The fingers pressed in hard until Quinn's lips puckered and his teeth gritted. Alan could not reach Quinn in time as Frank raised his bloody fist, balled it up, and smacked Quinn in the face, snapping his skull back over his shoulders.

"Smarts, doesn't it? Gettin' slammed in the nose fucks you all up. You got that pain shootin' through your brain. Your eyes fill up with water. It ain't any kind of fun."

"C'mon now Frank that's enough! How are we going to explain that?"

"That's easy: he tripped and fell into the table."

"The tape...Frank. This is not how we police!"

"Heh, we can edit. He's going to pay."

Quinn snapped his head forward. Before he could grasp his bearings, he felt Frank's shovel-sized hands upon the back of his collar.

"This interview is over," Frank said as he picked Quinn up like a rag doll.

"Whoa, whoa Frank! Where are you taking him?"

The tips of his shoes scraped against the floor. Quinn kept his mouth shut; there was no point catching another beating.

"Where are you taking him?" Alan asked again.

"Remember our old friend, the biker?" Frank said coldly.

"Crazy Eight? No, not him." Alan wanted to stop Frank. Alan knew deep down that he could not. Not a man that big and full of fury.

"No such luck, but we got one of his crew behind the bars."

"We can't put Quinn with one of them. Those bikers should be behind rubber walls, not iron bars."

Alan took hold of Quinn's arm firmly, not enough to cause discomfort. Alan looked Quinn up and down, noticing he was still wearing a belt.

"Now who's the killer, Frank?" Alan dropped his head downward, almost as if the solution was on the floor somewhere. After searching the floor that provided no answers, Alan could only draw his conclusion.

"I want nothing to do with this Frank; this is going too far. He's just a kid. Nobody deserves this." Alan let go of Quinn's arm and left him with a pat on the back to remember him by. "Sorry kid, let's hope you make it to the morning. I wish I could have been of more help." Alan gave Quinn one more look. It was almost as if it was the last time; there was no more he could do. He had seen others try to bring down Frank, only for them to leave in his place, never heard from again.

"Alan," said Frank as held onto Quinn's arm in one hand, reaching out for his partner the last ten years.

"We catch killers, not help to kill. I want nothing to do

with this. I ignored a lot of stuff over the past, not this, though. I want no part of this," replied Alan.

A pained look stretched across Frank's face.

"I'll write the report the way that will keep us clean."

Alan shook his head in disappointment, taking a deep look into Frank's eyes. He could not look into them for long. He never wanted to be this cop. A little hard, he had to be. Too much kindness was a weakness. He felt a little bit of that fresh-eyed kid, straight out of the academy with aspirations of saving the world, die a little inside with every year that passed since.

Frank called out, but Alan never responded, walking away as if a ghost, wandering away into the crowds of faceless criminals and forgotten justice.

Frank knew deep down that Alan would return to the fold: men like him always did.

It was a shame. Frank thought his efforts to groom an apprentice were working. Frank took comfort in the fact there was no dramatic handing in of the gun and badge, or maybe that was worse? Maybe he would go home and dwell upon it, only to leave a detailed report on the right desk ready for tomorrow.

"So are you going to show me to my room, Francis?"

"I've somebody I want you to meet. You know what...I'll leave it a couple of days before I notify your relatives." Frank continued to chuckle as if entertained by his own threatening wit. Quinn gave no resistance as Frank led him out of the room, down the narrow hallways and protesting screams of innocence and guilt, ignoring all the wild and inventive threats uttered by Frank. In the corner of this grey, concrete hell sat his bunk-buddy, who spoke through his gritted teeth.

"I'm gonna suck out ya eyeballs and skull fuck you stupid, badge-wearing pigs," bellowed a voice in the darkness.

"Play nice now," replied Frank as he grabbed Quinn's arm tighter, pinching at the flesh between thumb and forefinger.

Much to Frank's dissatisfaction, Quinn gave no response, not even a small recoil of his arm.

Frank shoved Quinn into the cell and slammed the door with an empty clang.

The cops of the day shift clocked off, exchanging tired greetings in the forms of nods and grunts with the night shift cops. Frank was amongst those cops. The comfort of his one-bedroom apartment beckoned. It would only be a matter of time before he really retired properly to the Florida Keys paid for by kickbacks, broken fingers and turning the odd blind eye for the right government official. Frank had only made a couple of stops on his way home. Another visit to the old Chinese man who winced as he handed over a day's pay. Frank gave no sympathy, leaving the old man with a cold warning about payments. There were, after all, worse people out there. They would not offer the protection he would.

Traffic was heavy tonight; the rain pattered against his window screen. Frank's window screen wipers kicked lazily into action, the gentle rubber squeaking relaxing him. There was a kind of peace between the rain and the road, a stark contrast to the other motorists honking their horns in anger in a hurry to get home. Taking his hands off the wheel, Frank reached into his glove compartment. He took off his beaten and scratched digital watch and exchanged it for another. He watched the stuck traffic for signs of movement as he put his other watch on. Frank brought his wrist up to his chest. His gold Rolex glimmered in the soft glows of rear view lights of those ahead. He would be home soon. Placing his hand back on the wheel, his foot ready to hit the gas as the traffic moved finally forward. The traffic slowly decongested. The cars now free. The honks of frustrated drivers drifted into silence, replaced by the gentle rumbles of engines. Frank put his foot down on the gas as he watched the storefronts and tenement buildings as he passed. All was quiet on the western front. After a couple of miles passed, he finally reached his destination. Frank pulled into the car park of the tenement building, home at last. He twisted the key in the ignition, and the engine fell silent. Frank sat for a moment, head tucked into his chest. Taking a deep breath, he ejected his seatbelt; it snapped back to its rightful place, ready again for use. Frank opened the car door, heaving himself out. Pulling his cell from his pocket, Frank noticed he had missed a couple of calls from both the station and Alan. Too late now, he was home. Whatever they wanted from him would have to wait until the morning.

Frank was too tired now to worry about the concerns of his partner. Perhaps Alan had changed his mind and realized that he could not fuck with the infinite. After all, it was a just balance, karmic. Frank dragged his body upwards to his sparsely furnished apartment; his feet felt heavy and ached. Frank unlocked his front door and flung it shut after he entered. He threw his keys onto the stand by the door. Frank threw himself into his big tattered chair. He reached over to the coffee table to grab his whiskey bottle and poured himself a glass. As the glass touched his lips, Frank's cell phone rang Again. Frank cussed and sighed as he flicked the phone open.

"What now? Can't you boys take a piss without needing me to hold your dick?"

"Alan's tried to ring you. We've tried to ring you. You're needed here now," replied the firm voice.

"Why? What is so bad that I am needed down there? I have just sat down after an eighteen-hour shift. My feet are killing me, I'm tired, I—"

"Your prisoners. Alan went down there to check on them; he found the biker and the other guy, dead. Alan's not happy. It's a mess down there."

"Okay, okay. Tell me what happened so I know what to

expect."

"You really should be down here seeing for yourself. Forensics cannot make a move until you are here. But seeing as Alan's on his way he can tell you."

"Tell me now!" barked Frank.

"Okay, okay. From how it looks, someone beat the biker to death. I mean he was almost beyond recognition, I don't think even God would have recognized him."

"The biker's dead?"

"Yep. Not just that, the other guy has hung himself from the bars by his belt. He's swinging like a damn piñata; there must have been one helluva fight. Quinn had long deep lacerations to his face and hands. We cannot cut him down for further examination until you get here. Somebody dropped the ball. Get down here as soon as Frank, we—"

Frank closed the phone before the conversation could run any further. The cogs in his turned into over-gear How was he going to explain this one? Who could he pitch the blame on? He should have just let it go. Things were slipping. Frank paced the small apartment from one end to the other. Never before had he had a prisoner die like this, let alone two? In the past people had caught beatings, everyone took a beating at some time.

Frank walked back over to the table on which the whiskey sat, pouring himself another glass. The whiskey flowed into the glass, swirling around as it hit the bottom. Before it had any real chance to settle, Frank shot his arm upwards, glass in hand, down the hatch it went, then another and another. With enough whiskey in his body to settle his nerves, Frank took a cigarette and placed it in his mouth. A knock at the door echoed around the room as he tried to light his cigarette.

"Hang on! I'll be there in a second," shouted Frank.

Only two or three people came to his door nowadays. None of them was welcome at this point if they ever were in the first place. The knock came again.

"Fucking wait, will ya!"

Frank approached the fish eye lens of his door. It was like looking through a drunken telescope. At first, there was a flicker of a shadow; there was movement somewhere out there.

"Who is it?"

The reply came in the form of a whistle of the wind and the pattering of rain.

"Who is it? You've been knocking on my door long enough."

Before Frank could walk away and get back in his seat, Alan came into view. His entire body was out of proportion in the fisheye lens, little head and large body. Frank's shoulders slumped, and a heavy sigh followed. Here Alan was to wax lyrical in his self-righteous way about the evils of corruption, Frank considered himself lucky that Alan had not ratted on him. So at least Frank could invite him in, give Alan a drink, and explain everything. Well, everything with a few lies intertwined with nuggets of truth. Frank opened the door. Alan stood there face sullen. Rain dripped off his coat onto the floor by the door. Frank would have greeted him with a used car salesman's smile, but now was not the time to act pleased.

"Don't stand there all day, come in for a minute. I need to talk to you before we shoot off."

"Okay," Alan muttered grimly as he shook the rainwater from his umbrella. Frank took a step back, allowing Alan to pass. Frank popped his head out of the door to see if there was anyone else out there. Bringing his head and body back in, Frank closed the door. Frank turned to Alan, who was still standing, awaiting further instruction.

"For the love of Christ, Alan, take a seat please."

Alan hoisted his coat to the sides before he sat; he steadied himself slowly into the chair. His every move was delicate as if Frank was to be treated like a dangerous explosive.

"Alan, just relax. Now we have a lot of ground to cover. I

am telling you now, I never meant for it to happen. It's tragic. I only wanted to wipe off that shit-eating grin. I only wanted him to catch a beating. To be taught a lesson. I've done a lot of bad things, I know; maybe this is a wakeup call. Just back me up on this, one time, and I'll go straight, promise."

Frank moved to the opposite side of the room where the whiskey sat. Alan's eyes followed him. Frank bent down to the whiskey bottle and grabbed another glass.

"Want a drink, Alan?"

"No thanks."

"Geez Alan, you're cranky. Have a drink, relax; we're on the same page now." The words slurred a little from Franks' lips. Frank turned his back, taking his time to fill both glasses with whiskey.

Frank muttered about mounting debts, the stress of the job, as he filled the glasses. Frank turned back to Alan; he walked over and handed Alan his drink. Frank walked back over to his own chair, his cogs turning quickly. Frank made himself comfortable, taking a sip from his drink. He looked Alan in the eyes. It took a moment or two to get his vision right: the alcohol had hit his system harder than he had realized.

"You've cost me a lot Frank; my entire life is now gone because of you," Alan said sternly.

Frank took a deep breath and then spoke.

"Don't worry Alan; you'll still have a job. You must trust me okay? I will make things right; I will make it so that none of this ever gets back to us. Now, where can I begin...?"

"You can begin to tell me what makes you and me so different?" asked Alan.

"Uh?" grunted Frank.

Alan leaned forward in his chair, placing his drink on the table before he continued.

"You know the greatest trick the devil ever performed, was

convincing the world he never existed..."

"What the hell are you on about...?"

It left Frank dumfounded. He looked closer at Alan

"No, no, no! It's not possible..."

Alan raised his hand, took hold of his face, and peeled the skin from his skull like a balaclava.

Alan's face fell to the floor, and Frank saw a grinning skinless face of contorted muscle and bloody gristle.

"Oh yes Frank, it is."

"Where?" Frank tried to catch a fleeting breath; his breathing came in short, quick stabs. "What? Where the hell is Alan?"

"Oh, they'll find Alan hanging around, if you'll forgive the pun."

Frank's drink dropped to the ground with an empty thud, the whiskey shooting out of the glass onto the floor. If Frank had neighbours, they would have heard his screams pierce the night.

No one answers screams until they fall silent.

No one ever saw Frank again.

The department gave Alan a fitting funeral service. They would remember him as a good cop, a hero to the downtrodden. The police never could keep those nights' events contained for long. Quinn, he would hunt. He would watch through the windows of his intended prey, with Frank's dirty money to help fund his new life. Unaware that Maker was watching him.

Here, far away from home among those smells and those voices, forever behind him.

Here and now, in death, not life, Quinn finally belonged.

Perceptions

BRYAN NICKELBERRY

Tahmid opens the door for me, and I walk into his home, taking in its details as he closes the door, then walks into the kitchen. The carpet is black, and well used, but not overly worn. The furniture is comfortable and high quality. There are pictures of Tahmid and/or his family on the walls and the mantel piece, but there aren't many of the "knick knacks" that I've seen in the houses of other students. Curious. And that smell...Then I notice that Tahmid is calling me. "Yes?" I say, turning around.

"I was just letting you know that the bathroom is down that hallway, and asking if you'd like something to drink," he says, before drinking a glass of water.

I consider. "Thank you and no thank you, respectively," I say. "Though I may accept water later. I hadn't realized your family originates in Egypt."

Tahmid nods as he re-enters the living room. "Yup, I'm first-generation American, but we go back to see the rest of the family often enough."

I consider that for a moment. "I've never been to Egypt. I'd like to go someday." Then I turn fully around. "The home you share with your parents looks...nice. I'll inspect the kitchen and the bathroom later, before I come to a final decision on it. Now, show me your room," I say, turning back to him. Tahmid just looks at me for a moment, then he begins laughing. I decide to wait until he's finished.

Once he finally stops, he looks at me and says slowly, "Theresa...could you sit down for a second? Please?" Seeing no reason not to, I sit in the chair that he indicates, finding myself perpendicular to him. "Thank you," he says. Then he stands up and begins pacing.

"You're anxious, Tahmid," I say. "Why?"

He stops pacing and looks at me. "Theresa..." he begins, moving his hands in circles to indicate his search for words. "You're amazing," he finally says. "You're smart, and beautiful, and a bit odd; but in a way that's actually kind of charming."

"Thank you," I say.

"And after years of wondering what was wrong with me, and why I couldn't get a date; after years of hoping that someone like you would walk into my life and notice me despite being short and compact, you actually did. You don't have a problem being seen in public with me, and I can't thank you enough for all of that," he says, hands falling to his sides as he looks at me with a half-smile.

"Alright," I say, still waiting for him to make a point.

"Crazier still, you don't ask about the injuries I come to school with, or the days that I miss—"

"It's simple Tahmid," I say, cutting to the point. "Your father beats you and your mother." I say. "There is no need for shame on your part."

Tahmid looks horrified and takes a step back. "No, he doesn't."

"Yes, Tahmid, he does." I say simply. "On regular occasions I catch the scent of stale blood on your body. I can actually taste it in the air when you're around. Then there are smells of odd chemicals, which leads me to deduce that your father also abuses prescription drugs. He may even be producing them here in the home, though I have yet to find evidence of such. Final evidence of this behavior is found in your dark-colored furniture and black carpet; both of which hide bloodstains well.

I must admit that I'm impressed by the sheer apparent level of his genius and violence toward you—"

"My father doesn't hit me!" he shouts. Then realizing he was shouting, he sits down, and laughs a bit as tears come to his eyes. "Actually it's just the opposite," Tahmid says, sitting back on the sofa, and holding his forehead. "He takes the worst hits for mom and I so that we don't have to. Heck, right now his arm is a barely-flexing mass of scar tissue, and his leg is *still* in a cast because of how bad he got it the last time." He says, shaking his head, and lowering his arm. "No Theresa, trust me," Tahmid says, "Mom and I get roughed up, but not by Dad. Never by dad."

"Oh. Well that's good to know—"

"And that's another thing Theresa," he says, sitting forward and steepling his fingers. "Ever since you came to programming 101, I've found myself telling you things about myself and my family," he says, standing up, and beginning to pace again. "Things I make it a point not to tell anyone. I don't know if that's just because I'm head over heels for you, or what, but...my family has secrets. Dangerous secrets..." he says. Then he puts his face in his hands and laughs some more. "Oh crap I sound like a cliché. How could this be going so badly, so quickly?" he asks.

"Both your confession of secrets and your difficulty in thinking are probably related to the pheromones I'm releasing," I say.

"Wait what?" he asks, looking at me askance.

"But I think your problem is rooted in your internal, mental conflict," I say. Then he looks up. "You just told me that you want to be friends at least and implied perhaps even sexual partners, while your hormones are suggesting you'd like to become permanent mates with me, but societal conventions—"

"What the hell?" Tahmid says, jaw dropping.

"Hell," I say. "A religious construct. Ah. If your religious preferences are the issue—"

He shakes his head quickly. "No, that's not the problem. We're Muslim actually, but no I'm not ruled by my religion. Dad brought Mom here to get her away from the extremism back home, and the only objection they'd have right now is the same objection every other parent would have to a pair of sixteen-year-olds having sex. And while I'm betting it would feel great, you wanting to go straight to my room and—"

"I want to see your room to learn more about you, not to mate," I say. "Also, I need to check your computer for its speed and operational parameters. Finally, you may have a closet, or a private bathroom I could live in, though I suppose I wouldn't be against copulation. I've never done so before. It could be stimulating on several levels, and would assuredly provide me with valuable information."

Tahmid just stares at me. "Uh..."

"But despite your admission of attraction," I say, crossing my arms, "you also seem to be on the verge of suggesting that we shouldn't even associate. That is the conflict I've been referring to. You yourself haven't decided which possibility you want; though you've narrowed it down to being friends, having intercourse with me, and asking me not to be involved with you beyond an acquaintance's familiarity—"

"Because I can't!" He shouts, throwing his arms wide open. "I can't decide! Frankly, you're right," he says, letting his arms flop to his sides. "You seem like a woman I'd love to marry someday, the perfect woman I've been praying to meet. And while sex in the meantime would be nice while we get our lives together—"

"Then we'll go topic by topic until you find answers," I say. "Do you want to have sex with me?" Tahmid just stops and looks at me.

After a few moments' concentration, he says, "For two weeks now, you've been very anxious to see my room, and now you're talking about living in it..."

"Yes," I say. "Because it's your room. It's full of information about you: sights, smells, stories. I find that seeing someone's room is one of the best ways to learn about that person. I'm considering living with you because I trust you. But there are still things you're hiding from me, which are preventing me from making a final decision. Then again I suppose intercourse would also be a good way—"

"Ok Theresa, stop," he says. After taking another moment to think, he sits down, looks me in the eyes and says, "I have a disease. It's very easy to transmit, and sex is one way of doing so, but I wouldn't want you to have to live with this. My disease brings a lot of the complications that put me in bandages, and the stuff that heals me or suppresses the disease makes me smell like chemicals sometimes; and I don't want you to be forced into dealing with those complications, especially the way all of us with the disease have to." Moving forward, Tahmid takes my hands in his and kneels before me. "Theresa...I think...I think I love you too much to put you through this," he says, looking down and shaking his head. "Maybe years from now, after we've graduated high school and college, and I don't know, if I somehow manage to find a way to make all of this...safer..."

"Explain your affliction to me in detail," I say, "And I will decide from there whether to involve myself with you further, or extricate myself from you. Honestly, it may be a non-issue."

Laughing bitterly, he stands up. "I wish it could be a non-issue, Theresa, I really do," he says. "But there are days when my whole family doesn't know whether we're going to make it home alive. I've been stabbed, bit, burned, mauled, partially frozen, electrocuted, shot—"

"If you can survive all of that along with a disease ravaging you from the inside, then neither of us will have a problem, Tahmid," I say.

He shakes his head and puts his head in his hands. "You're

not listening," he says, then he shakes his head quickly and looks into my eyes. "Why is it so hard to think around you? Why can't I say what I need to say?"

"Because my pheromones have you speaking everything on your mind, and it turns out you're looking for excuses, imagining worst case scenarios, and most likely worrying about nothing," I say. That's when he stops.

Frozen in place, he just stares at me. Then he slowly asks, "Why would you say that?"

"I said the first part because it's true. I said that you're likely worried about nothing," I say, looking him in the eyes, "Because I'm more than a bit of a survivor, and whatever this ailment may be, it hasn't killed you yet. Thus, I'll likely be fine."

"Worried...about nothing?" he asks. "*Worried about nothing?!*"

An explosion of yellow fur with black spots spreads from beneath his sweatshirt to cover his entire body, as his legs snap into a different shape, and his fingernails slide out into claws. A tail flies from beneath his sweatshirt, as his human teeth extend into the sharp teeth of a cat, and his mouth begins to pull forward, while his nose slides down. His muscle mass increases as I watch, while the pants and hooded sweatshirt which had been a bit big, become a bit too small and tight. A bone spike extends backward from the bottom of each wrist, as he steps out of his shoes, before stalking toward me on digitigrade legs.

"Worried about nothing?" the guttural voice asks, as tears leave tracks in his fur. "I can bench press a Geo Metro, but I can leg press an empty cargo container, Theresa!" he says, stopping inches from me, and looking me in the eyes. "I can run at 120 miles per hour for three hours before I collapse. My claws and fangs can rend core-ten steel, Theresa. I'm not as strong or as durable as other shifters, but I can tear a man in half with my bare hands, and I can heal from a shotgun blast to the heart and lungs in a few hours!" he says, coming to a panting halt. "I'm not human, Theresa; I'm a monster! My parents are too, but the things we deal with are worse! We regularly wind up in situations so heinous that we're not sure any of us will be coming back. It's what we signed on for by being born this way, and it's what we do to make sure the world keeps spinning without knowing we're here. Whatever you've survived until now, I promise you it pales compared to things that can put monsters into intensive care...or the ground." He slowly stops as I put the metal clasp I'd had around my pony tail onto the table. "Uh Theresa..." he says much more quietly, taking a step back as my hair wakes up and begins to explore the chair, "What—"

"You're not a monster Tahmid," I say. "Being monstrous is a state of mind, not a state of physical being; and you fall markedly short of that mindset. I'd believed your father matched the definition, but with this new information, I am re-assessing that conclusion. As to my hair clasp, if you remember when you asked me about it a few weeks ago, I said that my hair gets a bit...unruly without it," I say. "You said that you were born with your condition which implies you may have been lying about its transmitability, though even if you weren't, I'm not certain I can catch mammalian diseases," I say. Then I close my eyes, sigh, and lean back as the chlorophyll returns to the surface of my skin. "I hope you don't mind," I say as the light moss forming my shirt and the leaves forming my pants begin to dry and flake off. "But I spend too much time crammed into this lesser form. It's always nice to stretch out, and if you've done so, then I will too."

The flaps of skin over each of my shoulders unhook, and my upper torso spreads open as my trunk extends. My arms unfold, and the small hook-like thorns on their undersides open, as the ring and index fingers on each of my hands retract, and the remaining fingers elongate. The skin on my legs dries and shrinks back to its original woody texture as my legs begin to segment, and my neck lengthens. I feel my pupils expand to envelop the rest of each eye, and with the flaps on my body open, my sense of smell comes back to full strength.

As I begin to differentiate between the other assorted scents present, I notice the smell of fear in the air and open my eyes to see Tahmid with his ears lowered, several feet away, and near the door. Shifting my vision from ultraviolet to infrared, I can see how fast his heart is beating.

"Well…" he says after a few quiet seconds, "I…have to admit. I wasn't expecting you to unfold into a…plant? Mantis? Hybrid?"

I look down, taking in my system of interlocking root tendrils where legs used to be, and the extra segments in my elongated arms. I would agree to the plant-like nature of my body, but it takes a slight change in thought to understand how and why he would compare me to a praying mantis. Could it really be as simple as the green coloration, large eyes, and extra arm joints?

Switching pheromones causes the bees within me to stir. They take to the air; exploring the house, and bringing me more information. "I have to admit," I say, looking back at him, "I hatched alone; so I can't tell you exactly what I am. That's a large part of why I made the trek from South America to Puyallup, Washington. I needed a quiet place, with good soil, where I could learn about the world, my place in it, and myself. And all of this without an overabundance of questions, as long as the proper paperwork was provided. This place fit those parameters quite nicely. Furthermore," I say, rising from the chair, and beginning to move toward him, "I am impressed. You did actually worry me a bit with regard to our potential future relationship before you revealed your transformation. I'm still learning about emotional responses, and you worked one out of me. But now that I've seen your secret," I say smiling as I move closer and release still more calming and complacency pheromones into the air. "I agree with my previous assessment: There's absolutely nothing to worry about," I say, wrapping an arm around him. "Now, let's discuss these dangerous and harmful situations you find yourself in."

Bios

Clint Collins's horror fiction can be found in the very first Horror Writers Association anthology, *Under the Fang*, and other anthologies such as *Fifty Shades of Decay*, *Bill of Frights*, *Cthulhurotica*, *Transformed*, and *Haunted*. Clint also co-edited the anthology *Snowpocalypse*, featuring stories of an endless winter. Having been an editor for both the US government and private industry, Clint now lives in Indiana, a state where ghosts patiently wait in abandoned farmhouses and mysterious rituals occur deep in late-summer cornfields.

Steve Dillon writes dark horror fiction often with surreal elements, and these have mostly published in the *Things in the Well* series of themed anthologies. He's also published two collections of short fiction and poetry, "The Beard and Other Weirdness" and "Deeper, Darker Things and Other Oddities". His latest work consists of 10 drabbles and double-drabbles and these can be found in the erotic horror anthology "Guilty Pleasures and Other Dark Delights".

http://facebook.com/SteveDillonWriter will connect you to him, or visit ThingsInTheWell.com

Shaun Horton is the author of the sci-fi/horror novels Hannah and Class 5, as well as the cryptid horror Cenote. He writes from the beautiful pacific northwest, crammed between the city of Seattle and the woods of the Olympic National Forest. His favorite monsters are actually the giant, city-crushing ones like Godzilla, but all are fair game. You can learn more about him on his blog, or on Goodreads.

https://www.goodreads.com/author/show/7031768.Shaun_Hort

on
https://shaunhorton.blogspot.com/

Roger Jackson lives in England, existing mainly on a diet of Horror and energy drinks. Stories have crawled from the graveyard of his brain for as long as he can remember, with many of them finding a home in fanzines, magazines, UK radio and anthologies full of nightmare fuel. He likes how writing about himself in the third person sounds like an obituary.

Bryan Nickelberry was born in the dark and rain of the Pacific Northwest. He spent most of his life gathering stories via all mediums, before beginning to tell some of his own.

Rebecca Rowland is an editor, librarian, and author who specializes in dark fiction. Her stories most recently appeared in the anthologies *Strange Stories, The Year's Best Hardcore Horror (vol 4)*, and *Ghosts, Goblins, Murder, and Madness*. Her first short fiction collection, *The Horrors Hiding in Plain Sight*, was published by Dark Ink Books in 2018 and her first novel, Pieces, penned with writing partner Michael Aloisi, was released in 2019. Despite her love of the ocean and unwavering distaste for cold temperatures, she currently resides in a landlocked and often icy corner of New England. See what mayhem she's plotting next at RowlandBooks.com.

Steven Van Patten is a celebrated writer and Brooklyn native. *His Brookwater's Curse* trilogy features an 1860s Georgia plantation slave who becomes law enforcement within the vampire community. His *Killer Genius* series is about a hyper intelligent black woman who uses high-end technology as a socially conscious serial killer.

SVP's short fiction includes contributions to horror anthologies like *Hell's Kitties* and the Stoker Award nominated

New York State of Fright. A collection of short horror and dark fiction stories entitled *Hell At The Way Station*, published by Laughing Black Vampire Productions and co-authored by acclaimed storyteller, Marc Abbott hit shelves in 2019.

Along with a plethora of honors and accolades, SVP recently won three African-African-American Literary Awards, two for Hell At The Way Station (Best Anthology and Best In Science Fiction in 2019) and one for Best Independent Publisher.

He uses his full name on Facebook but goes by @svpthinks on Twitter and Instagram. When he's not creating macabre literature, he can be found stage managing television shows primarily in New York City and occasionally on the West Coast. Along with being a member of the New York Chapter of The Horror Writer's Association, he's also a member of The Director's Guild of America and professional arts fraternity Gamma Xi Phi. His website is www.laughingblackvampire.com.

Originally from Escanaba, Michigan, **Kate Watts** currently lives in Alabama with her husband, son, and an array of pets. She likes ghost stories, Weimar cinema, fantastic art, and contemplating the weird coincidences inherent in everything. She also likes every kind of cat except one: Dr. Seuss' Cat in the Hat, who terrified her as a child, and whom she has depicted in the story included here as the Lovecraftian agent of chaos he really is.